Crime Where the
Nights are Long

Dedicated
to
JOHN ROBERT COLOMBO
who has shown the way

Crime Where the Nights are Long

Canadian Stories of Crime, Adventure, and Terror
from the Golden Age of Storytelling

Edited by
David Skene-Melvin

SIMON & PIERRE
A MEMBER OF THE DUNDURN GROUP
TORONTO · OXFORD

Design: Scott Reid
Printer: Friesens Corporation

Canadian Cataloguing in Publication Data

Crime where the nights are long: Canadian stories of crime and adventure
from the golden age of storytelling

ISBN 0-88924-281-X

1. Detective and mystery stories, Canadian (English).* 2. Canadian fiction (English) — 19th century.* 3. Canadian fiction (English) — 20th century.* I. Skene-Melvin, David, 1936–

PS8323.D4C745 1999   C813'.087208   C98-931583-5
PR9197.35.D48C74 1999

1 2 3 4 5   03 02 01 00 99

THE CANADA COUNCIL | LE CONSEIL DES ARTS
FOR THE ARTS | DU CANADA
SINCE 1957 | DEPUIS 1957

We acknowledge the support of the **Canada Council for the Arts** for our publishing program. We also acknowledge the support of the **Ontario Arts Council** and the **Book Publishing Industry Development Program** of the **Department of Canadian Heritage.**

Care has been taken to trace the ownership of copyright material used in this book. The author and the publisher welcome any information enabling them to rectify any references or credit in subsequent editions.

J. Kirk Howard, President

Printed and bound in Canada.

Printed on recycled paper.

Simon & Pierre
8 Market Street
Suite 200
Toronto, Canada
M5E 1M6

Simon & Pierre
73 Lime Walk
Headington, Oxford,
England
OX3 7AD

Simon & Pierre
2250 Military Road
Tonawanda NY
U.S.A. 14150

Contents

Acknowledgements

I could not have compiled this anthology without the help of Richard Bleiler and Stephen Davies, to whom I am most grateful for their suggestions and information, or the typing skills of Diane Schwartz and Sharon Smith, and, of course, the support and comfort of my wife, Ann.

INTRODUCTION

The period from the early 1880s through the First World War has been called "The Age of the Storytellers." The intention of the writers of this period was not to write great literature, but to entertain, spinning yarns to be printed and read, just as their predecessors, the minstrels and bards, recited and were listened to. Through their countless tales of adventure and derring-do, they brought romance and colour to the lives of those who could do more than dream. This was the age of Sir Arthur Conan Doyle, H. Rider Haggard, Rudyard Kipling, Robert Louis Stevenson, and H. G. Wells. Canadian writers contributed in no small way to the cornucopia of romance and adventure the reading public could find at the newsstands and bookstores. Messrs. Roper, Beharriell, and Scheider in *Literary History of Canada: Canadian Literature in English* (Second edition, 1976) say "the Canadian fiction-writers between 1880 and 1920 were read more widely by their contemporaries, inside and outside Canada, than have been the Canadian fiction-writers — collectively — since."

We have garnered from amongst the collections and magazines produced from the Late Victorian Era up through the introduction of the "Pulps" in the 1920s a selection of choice nuggets from the rich mother lode of popular fiction by Canadian writers. Herein you will find stirring tales by W.H. Blake, Susan Carleton, W.H. Drummond, W.A. Fraser, Sir Gilbert Parker, Hesketh Prichard, R.T.M. Scott, Alan Sullivan, and Lillian Benyon Thomas. Some have never been anthologized before; all are guaranteed to set the blood a-racing and stimulate the imagination. Crime and its detection are related in W.A. Fraser's "The Gold Wolf," Hesketh Prichard's "The Crime at Big Tree Portage," and R.T.M. Scott's "Bombay Duck." In this anthology, we have widened the scope to include not just tales of adventure and crime, but of terror and horror as well. The power of guilt and the revenge of the grave is recounted in Sir Gilbert Parker's "The Flood." Ghostly apparitions are introduced in Susan Carleton's "The Clasp of Rank" and Lillian Benyon Thomas's "When Wires are Down." Canada has its own indigenous monsters, the most terrifying being the Wendigo and in this anthology the supernatural is further explored with the presentation of two expositions of this hideous creature, one in prose, W.H. Blake's "A Tale of the Grand Jardin," and one in poetry, W.H. Drummond's "The Windigo." The authoritative text on this legendary monster is John Robert Colombo's *Wendigo: An Anthology of Fact and Fantastic Fiction*, originally published by Western Producer Prairie Books in Saskatoon, Saskatchewan, in 1982. This highly readable collection of descriptions and discussions of the appearances of the Wendigo, the Algonkian spirit of cannibalism and selfishness, is highly recommended to anyone interested in the genre of horror fiction or the folklore of North America's Native peoples. It is available in an expanded edition with an appendix of new material from Colombo & Company, 42 Dell Park Ave, Toronto, Ontario, M6B 2TC ($40.00, ISBN 1-896308-35-X). Another Canadian monster is the "*loup garou*," the French-Canadian version of the werewolf, and is encountered in Alan Sullivan's chilling story "The Eyes of Sebastien."

BOMBAY DUCK
R(eginald) T(homas) M(aitland) Scott, 1882–1966.

Ontario-born in the town of Woodstock on August 14, 1882, R.T.M. Scott was educated at Woodstock College — in its day one of the most highly respected preparatory schools, if not in the same social milieu of Upper Canada College — and from 1901 to 1904 at the Royal Military College (RMC) at Kingston, Ontario. From 1908 to 1912, he worked as an engineer for the International Marine Signal Company installing marine lighting in Italy, Arabia, India, Burma, Ceylon, and Australia. In 1914, he accepted a captain's commission in the Twenty-first Battalion, Canadian Expeditionary Force (CEF). He saw active service on the Western Front in Belgium, subsequently attaining the rank of major. From 1919, he lived in New York City where he died on February 5, 1966. He created Aurelius Smith, a New York City-based private investigator, in a series of short stories with a psychic element for the "slicks," (e.g., *The Saturday Evening Post*) as opposed to the pulps. Scott was not without merit and ability and his best work lies in his short stories.

In the 1930s, his son, R.T. Scott II, created for the pulps Richard Wentworth — "The Spider" — in works often erroneously attributed to his father.

Secret Service Smith. New York: Dutton, 1923. Short stories.
The Black Magician. New York: Dutton, 1925. Novel.
Ann's Crime. New York: Dutton, 1926. Also published as *Smith of the Secret Service.* London: Amalgamated, 1929. Novel.
Aurelius Smith — Detective. New York: Dutton, 1927. Short stories.
The Mad Monk. New York: Kendall, 1931. Novel.
Murder Stalks the Mayor. London: Rich, 1935. Novel
The "Agony Column" Murders: A Secret Service Smith Novel. New York: Dutton, 1946. Novel.
The Nameless Ones: A Secret Service Smith Novel. New York: Dutton, 1947.

THE CLASP OF RANK
S. Carleton, pseudonym of Susan Carleton (Morrow) Jones, (Mrs. Guy Carleton), 1869–1926.

Born and educated in Halifax, Nova Scotia, where she was a lifelong resident, Susan Jones wrote novels and short stories for the pulps under the bylines of S. Carleton, Guy Carleton, Helen Milicente, Carleton-Milicente, and S. Carleton Jones. She was the sister-in-law of both the poetess Frances Bannerman and the novelist Alice Jones, both daughters of Alfred G. Jones, lieutenant-governor of Nova Scotia from 1900 to 1906.

A Detached Pirate: The Romance of Gay Vandeleur. As by Helen Milicente. London: Greening, 1900.
A Girl of the North: A Story of London and Canada. As by Helen Milicente. London: Greening, 1900.
The Career of Mrs. Osborne. As by Carleton-Milicente. New York: Smart Set, 1903.
The Micmac: or, "The Ribboned Way." As by S. Carleton. New York: Holt, 1904.
Out of Drowning Valley. As by S. Carleton Jones. New York: Holt, 1910.

The LaChance Mine Mystery. As by S. Carleton. Toronto: McClelland & Stewart, 1920.

The Forest Runner. As by S. Carleton. London: Melrose, 1925.

THE CRIME AT BIG TREE PORTAGE
Hesketh (Vernon Hesketh) Prichard, 1876–1922.

We have cheated in including Prichard because he is not a Canadian, but his character, November Joe, most certainly is. Born in India, Prichard was taken as an infant to England by his widowed mother. He spent most of his life travelling and hunting and used his outdoor experiences as background for his serial novel, *November Joe: Detective of the Woods*, recounting the adventures of possibly the only backwoods detective in the literature of the genre, from which we have abstracted the introductory story. Prichard collaborated with his mother, Kate Ryall Prichard, on many works, notably those featuring "Don Q," Don Quebranta Huesos, about whom there are two collections of short stories: *The chronicles of Don Q* (1904), and *The New Chronicles of Don Q* (1906 US title, *Don Q in the Sierra*), and one novel, *Don Q's Love Story* (1909).

THE EYES OF SEBASTIEN
(Edward) Alan Sullivan, 1868–1947.

Alan Sullivan was born in Montreal on November 29, 1868, the son of the Right Reverend Edward Sullivan, Bishop of Algoma, and Frances Mary (Renaud) Sullivan, but grew up in Sault Ste. Marie, Ontario. He was educated at Loretto College School in Scotland, Ontario, and graduated in Civil Engineering from the University of Toronto. He then worked in the Algoma District of Northern Ontario as an engineer for twenty years before becoming a full-time writer. He was a past president of the Arts & Letters Club of Toronto. During World War I, he was a captain in the RAF. He died on August 6, 1947, at the age of 78 at Tilford House, Farnham, Surrey, England — the home of his son-in-law, Captain Basil Liddell-Hart, the noted British military commentator. He also wrote under the pseudonym Sinclair Murray.

Cariboo Road: A Novel. Toronto: Nelson, 1946. Set in the Cariboo country of the British Columbia interior during the 1860s gold rush.

The Jade God. London: Bles, 1924.
The Passing of Oul-i-But and Other Tales. London: Dent, 1913.
Under the Northern Lights. London: Dent, 1926.

Sullivan wrote 31 other novels under his own name, the most famous of which are *The Rapids* (1922), a fictionalized account of the industrialization of Sault Ste. Marie, and *Three Came to Ville Marie* (1941), for which he won a Governor General's Literary Award for Fiction, as well as the useful *Aviation in Canada, 1917–18* (1919), and twelve novels under the name Sinclair Murray, several of which deal with the paranormal.

THE FLOOD
Sir (Horatio) Gilbert Parker, baronet, 1862–1932.

An historian and novelist, Gilbert Parker was born in Camden East, Addington, northeast of Napanee, Ontario, on November 23, 1862, the eldest son of Joseph Parker. Educated locally and at the Ottawa Normal School, he taught school locally, then attended Trinity University (now Trinity College, University of Toronto), in Toronto where he studied theology. In 1886, he set out for the South Seas and Australia, eventually fetching up in England in 1889, where he established himself as a journalist and latterly became MP for Gravesend in the House of Commons from 1900 to 1918. He was knighted in 1902, made a baronet in 1915, and became a member of the Privy Council in 1916. During the First World War, he was in charge of propaganda aimed at North America. He died in London, England on September 6, 1932, but is buried in Canada.

The Chief Factor: A Tale of the Hudson's Bay Company. New York: Trow Directory Co., 1892.
Pierre and His People: Tales of the Far North. Toronto: Copp Clark, 1897.
An Adventurer of the North: Being a Continuation of the Histories of "Pierre and His People" and the Latest Existing Records of Pretty Pierre. London: Methuen, 1895.
A Romany of the Snows: Second Series of "An Adventurer of the North", Being a Continuation of "Pierre and His People." Toronto: Copp Clark, 1898.

Northern Lights. Toronto: Copp Clark, 1909.

Among his other thirty-five fiction and non-fiction works, Parker's best-known novel is *The Seats of the Mighty: Being the Memoirs of Captain Robert Moray, Some Time an Officer in the Virginia Regiment, and Afterwards of Amherst's Regiment* (London: Methuen, 1896), for donkey's years a staple textbook in secondary school English in Canada.

THE GOLD WOLF
William Alexander Fraser, 1859–1933.

Born at River John in Pictou County, Nova Scotia, in 1859, William Fraser received his early education in New York City and Boston, but at 14 he returned to Canada to live with an uncle in Elgin County in Southwestern Ontario. He graduated in engineering and helped to develop the early oil wells in Western Ontario. Subsequently, he spent seven years prospecting for oil in Burma and in India, where he became a lifelong friend of Rudyard Kipling. Fraser returned to Canada and spent six years prospecting for oil in Western Canada where, in the employ of the Canadian government, he sank the first well at Pelican Falls, Alberta, and latterly prospected for precious metals in the Cobalt District of Northern Ontario in its roaring days. Due to illness, he gave up field work and settled in Georgetown, Ontario, where he lived for many years. Late in his life he moved to Toronto, where he died in his residence in his seventy-fifth year on November 9, 1933. It was Fraser who suggested and saw into realization the Silver Cross for mothers whose sons had died in the First World War. Fraser spun exciting tales with a humorous touch about exotic places as well as more sophisticated mysteries about horse racing. He was also a prolific writer of short stories, having over 250 to his credit.

The Blood Lilies. Toronto: Briggs, 1903.
Brave Hearts. New York: Scribner's, 1904. Horse-racing mystery.
Bulldog Carney. Toronto: McClelland & Stewart, 1919.
Caste. Toronto: Doran, 1922.
Delihah Plays the Ponies. Toronto: Musson, 1927. Horse-racing mystery.
The Eye of a God and Other Tales of East and West. New York:

Doubleday, 1899.

Red Meekins. Toronto: McClelland & Stewart, 1921. Set in the Cobalt District of Northern Ontario.

Thirteen Men. New York: Appleton, 1906.

Thoroughbreds. Toronto: George N. Morang, 1902. Horse-racing mystery.

The Three Sapphires. Toronto: McClelland, Goodchild & Stewart, 1918.

Fraser published five other books, both novels and collections of short stories.

A TALE OF THE GRAND JARDIN
William Hume Blake, 1861–1924.

A grandson of the famous Edward Blake, William Blake was born in Toronto, educated at the University of Toronto, and called to the bar in 1885. In addition to his collection of essays and short stories, *Brown Waters and Other Sketches* (1915), he also published another collection, *In a Fishing Country* (1922), both written to express his appreciation of the Laurentian landscape and to acquaint English readers with the customs and attitudes of the Québécois *habitants*. He also published the philosophical *A Fisherman's Creed* (1923). Blake is best known for his translations into English of Louis Hemon's *Maria Chapdelaine*, published in 1921, and Adjutor Rivard's *Chez nous [our Quebec home]* (1924).

THE WINDIGO
William Henry Drummond, 1854–1907.

Born at Currawn House, near Mohill, Country Leitrim, Ireland, Drummond immigrated to Montreal with his parents when he was 10. He attended Montreal High School, McGill University, and Bishop's University in Lennoxville, Quebec, from which he received his MD degree in 1884. He practised medicine in Montreal and died of a stroke in Cobalt, Ontario, where he was helping to control a smallpox outbreak at a mine owned by his brothers. His distinctive dialect verse, most of it amusing and most of it dealing with French-Canadian *habitant* life, was Canada's most popular poetry at the turn of the century.

WHEN WIRES ARE DOWN
Lillian Benyon Thomas

Regrettably, nothing is known of this authoress other than that she was Canadian, wrote short fiction for the pulps, and was a playwright writing a well-constructed comedy, *Jim Barber's Spite Fence*, in 1935. (*The Oxford Companion to Canadian History and Literature*. Edited by Noah Story. Toronto: Oxford University Press, 1967. p. 224.)

BOMBAY DUCK

by
R.T.M. Scott
from *The World's Best One Hundred Detective Stories* (in ten
volumes). Edited by Eugene Thwing. New York: Funk & Wagnalls,
1929. Volume Five

Messrs. Jacques Barzun and Wendell Hertig Taylor in their *A Catalogue of Crime*, (2nd imp. corr., New York: Harper & Row, 1971), credit the Aurelius Smith stories with managing "a trick or two worthy of Holmes" and offering "amusing sidelights on the New York of 1925," This opinion was seconded by Will Murray in *Twentieth-Century Crime and Mystery Writers*, (NY: St. Martin's; 1980), who said that "Bombay Duck," perhaps Scott's best story, "is a superb exercise in psychological manipulation."

This page intentionally left blank

Aurelius Smith, as he sat at tea with his secretary and versatile assistant, did not look very much like a detective, yet there was something calculatingly cool and deliberate about each trivial motion that he made. His old blue dressing gown, which he persistently refused to throw away, wrapped his long and lanky body in many angles as he sprawled ridiculously in his chair. His slender fingers dropped a slice of lemon into his cup with the deliberate motion of science. Bernice Asterley watched her employer with considerable interest — much more interest than a young woman usually gives to a man who takes tea in a perfectly impossible old blue dressing gown.

Langa Doonh, native servant from India, brought fresh muffins just as the doorbell sounded. Smith glanced at the muffins, but the urge for tobacco brought a black briar from his pocket, and he wandered lazily to the front window and stuffed dark shreds into the bowl as he stared moodily into Fenton Street, tiny one-block offshoot of Fifth Avenue. Few New Yorkers know Fenton Street, with its little colony of artists and students of strange things.

Bernice watched the back of the old dressing gown at the window and noted that a frayed blue cord permitted what was once a tassel to trail upon the floor. She turned back to the table when Langa Doonh came from the front door with letters that the letter carrier had left. Smith too turned his attention again to the table, but he merely glanced at the addresses on the envelopes and took up his cup without seeming to see the muffins. Bernice thought that he lived on tobacco except when Langa Doonh cooked a curry.

There was a continued silence, and Langa Doonh, quite satisfied that he had toasted sufficient muffins, took his departure to do some marketing for dinner. The little household was so well acquainted that words were almost unnecessary.

A few minutes later the bell sounded again, and this time Bernice went to the door while Smith stood with his back to the table and watched her leave the room. She returned a moment later with a man who followed her too closely to permit the formality of being announced. Nor did he wait for that formality after entering the room, but jerked a gun from his side pocket and pointed it threateningly toward Smith.

At sight of the gun Smith staggered backward against the table and threw an arm behind him for support. His hand, outstretched, plunged into his tea, and the cup crashed to the floor while he shook the hot liquid from his fingers and wiped them frantically upon his dressing gown. An expression of genuine fear and consternation overspread the face of Bernice as she saw her employer so visibly affected. Never before had she known his iron nerve to collapse in the face of danger. It was his collapse, rather than the threatening gun, which set her trembling a little to one side of the two men.

Up to this moment not a word had been spoken, but the stranger ended the silence. His was a cool and cutting voice, insolent in its indifference. Indeed, it seemed to Bernice that it was somewhat the voice of Smith himself when in a fighting mood — utterly devoid of emotion, cold, unconcerned.

"Very pretty acting," remarked the stranger, with the assurance of the slightest of sneers, "but your servant has just left the house and the broken cup will call no help."

But Bernice knew that Smith was aware of Langa Doonh's having left the house. She knew that he had not upset the cup to call assistance. She gained control of herself and watched, with apprehension, the powerful man behind the pistol while his dark eyes ran swiftly about the room.

"Uh-huh," said Smith by way of conversation after a considerable pause, and there was some relief for Bernice in the calmness of his blue-grey eyes.

Suddenly the stranger stepped up to Smith and pulled the long cord from the loops of his dressing gown. He pushed a chair against a radiator and indicated it to Smith, who sat down lazily but obediently. Rapidly the intruder ran the cord around Smith's arms and chest and tied him to the coils in the rear. He seemed ambidextrous as he shifted the gun from hand to hand and watched Bernice during the operation.

And during what followed there was no opportunity for her to be other than a spectator and it was only a matter of a few minutes before the man had gone. During those minutes he swiftly searched the room, pulling out many drawers and paying, perhaps, more attention to the typewriter desk of Bernice than to anything else. His keen eyes never remained away from Bernice for many seconds, and frequently he glanced at Smith while he searched. For a moment he stopped and scrutinized a small Hindu god before which Langa Doonh frequently burned incense.

"Ganesh!" he exclaimed and turned to Smith with a smile that cloaked part of a sneer. "The elephant-headed god must account for your success."

But Smith appeared too bored to reply, and the man strolled over to the tea table and glanced at the letters, picking up one in a blue envelope only to drop it again into the spilled tea. Once more he approached Smith and ran his hands into the dressing-gown pockets before backing to the door and stepping swiftly out. A moment later there was the sound of a departing motor.

Bernice was at the window in a flash, but failed to read the number of the departing car. She turned back into the room and stamped her foot in vexation.

"Put it over us completely!" she exclaimed.

Smith grinned, and his long legs straightened while his binding snapped as he rose to his feet.

"Thought I knew the tensile strength of that old cord," he

remarked as he took the rope rather tenderly in his hands and proceeded to tie it together again.

"But — but what did he want?" asked Bernice, looking in amazement at the broken cord. "He took nothing."

"He was clever, but he failed to find what he wanted," returned Smith. "From the window I saw him waiting in a car and watching the avenue corner — where the letter carrier turns. Of course I did not know he was waiting for the letter carrier, and I did not expect him to come in here."

"Well?" queried Bernice as Smith refilled his pipe and kicked the broken cup under the table.

"He's a killer," remarked Smith between puffs. "Thin, cruel lips and the eyes of a fanatic! Cool and cunning as he is merciless! Good thing he didn't come to kill. Might not have been so easy to handle."

"Easy to handle!" exclaimed Bernice. "It seems to me that he did all the handling."

"Thought he did," returned Smith, looking quizzically at his assistant. "You won the trick when the expression of your face convinced him that I had lost my nerve. It was the best acting you ever did."

For a moment the girl stared at the lanky man with the pipe. Her face crimsoned, and she looked uncomfortable.

"Ah, well," remarked Smith, as though talking to the pipe that he held in his long fingers, "I suppose a man must appear rather a helpless creature in the eyes of his secretary."

"You are in one of your tantalizing moods!" exclaimed Bernice, stamping her foot for the second time. "I don't believe you have any idea what the man came for."

"Maybe so and maybe not so," retorted Smith. "He waited for the letter carrier and therefore came for a letter — a blue letter like the one he tossed back into the spilled tea. There were seven letters, and I could guess the contents of six by a glance at the envelopes."

Bernice snatched up the letters and counted them. There were six.

"The seventh," said Smith, "I managed to secrete under my dressing gown during the process of sticking my hand into the tea and wiping it dry again."

"Oh!" ejaculated Bernice as Smith drew a blue envelope from under his arm.

The letter was both brief and unusual. It was addressed to Aurelius Smith and read:

> Dear Sir:
> Please come at once and discover the murderer
> of Richard. I shall await you, if necessary, until quite
> late this evening.

The letter was signed by Sybla Fanhaven.

"Wealthy woman," muttered Smith. "Fashionable address. Dictated to secretary, in all probability, since the body of it is typewritten." He scrutinized the signature closely. "Old woman, but full of energy. Eccentric. Strong will. Humph!"

"What do you make of it?" asked Bernice.

"Doubly interesting because of our recent visitor with the gun," returned Smith. "I think the case will be short and swift and will probably end — in death."

"Can I go with you?" asked Bernice.

Smith's eyes showed, at their corners, a faint smile of appreciation, but he walked over to the mantlepiece without answering and took up the little Hindu god.

"Old Ganesh," he soliloquized. "He knew you for the Hindu god of wisdom — god of luck to most natives. He must know India. Devilish mean man to handle. Hope you will give me some of your luck."

Gently he replaced the image and walked slowly from the room with his head bowed in thought.

And Bernice knew that she was to be left behind.

It was a large library into that Smith was shown shortly after the sun had set. A single lamp upon a table dimly revealed the fact that the four walls were lined with books from floor to ceiling, except where two large pictures, two windows, and a pair of sliding doors broke the array of literature. Beside the table were a man and a woman in evening dress. The woman, though quite "old," had the skin and eyes of youth beneath her white hair. The man was the man who had called upon Smith that afternoon with a gun.

"Ah, Mr. Smith," exclaimed the woman vivaciously, extending her hand without rising, "you came quickly. I should have invited you to dinner, but you will join us, anyway."

"Thank you," said Smith, taking the outstretched hand without appearing to notice the man with the black eyes.

"There will be only the three of us. Do you know that you almost kissed my hand?"

"You held your hand," replied Smith, "as only a woman who has lived much abroad can hold it."

He was looking, with polite indifference, at the man as he spoke.

"Gregory," she said, "I hope he likes curry." She turned back to Smith. "This is Mr. Gregory Avondale."

The dark-eyed man rose from his chair and there was just the fleeting hint of a sneer as he smiled pleasantly and extended his hand. Another instant and he bit his lip slightly as he met Smith's grasp. In shaking hands the man who exerts the first pressure gains a terrible advantage, and the long fingers of the blue-eyed man put forth the unexpected and surprising strength that lay in them. It was a declaration of war on the part of Smith.

"Mrs. Fanhaven," said Smith, dropping the rather limp hand, "you wrote me regarding the death of Richard."

She left her chair immediately and crossed the room almost with the grace of a young girl. Concealed lights flooded the room and revealed details that had been in shadow. Beneath a bird cage, suspended near a window, she pointed upward.

"Poor boy!" she said very simply.

Smith's face was quite blank of expression as he crossed the room and looked down upon a dead canary lying upon the bottom of the cage. He turned his eyes a little and looked into those of the woman who had summoned him. Self-control was what he saw and joy of life and perfect honesty capable of defying consequences. If sorrow were there, it was hidden by the courage of the grande dame — that courage that meets the great and the little equally.

"Last night," she said, "somebody strangled Richard. Poor boy! I must know who did it."

Gently Smith raised a hand and attempted to open the little sliding door of the cage. The catch stuck, and the cage swayed upon the suspending chain.

"Good!" said Smith. "The murderer steadied the cage with his left hand while he opened the door with his right. The projecting bottom of the cage would have been seized by the left hand with the fingers on top and the thumb underneath. The top surface is rough and will not take an impression, but the bottom surface is smooth.

Tomorrow I shall photograph the bottom of the cage and show you the thumbprint of the murderer."

"Exceedingly clever," said Avondale, strolling over to join them. "I opened the cage in just that way myself when I examined the bird this morning."

"Uh-huh," said Smith and questioned Mrs. Fanhaven. "This bird was a good singer and always sang at night if the lights were turned on suddenly?"

"Always," agreed Mrs. Fanhaven quickly.

"This library is on the second floor," commented Smith, staring slowly about the room. "Your bedroom, madam? It is also on this floor, is it not? You could hear the bird sing from your bedroom? You are a light sleeper?"

"Yes, yes, yes," answered Mrs. Fanhaven, watching Smith's face with keen interest. "I like the way you work."

The tall investigator shrugged his shoulders slightly and went back to the table, where he took up a telephone and called his Fenton Street number. Out of the corner of his eye he glimpsed Avondale, who seemed considerably interested in what was to be said over the wire.

"Oh, Bernice," he spoke shortly. "I forgot my gun. Bring it over to Mrs. Fanhaven's house at eleven. You will finish those notes by half past ten. Yes — at eleven." He turned directly to Avondale, looking at him over the top of the telephone. "I want my heavy automatic."

"How interesting!" exclaimed Mrs. Fanhaven, coming back to the table as quickly as she had left it. "I love to be on the right side in a drama."

"If you send for a heavy automatic in the case of a dead canary," remarked Avondale, lighting a cigarette and puffing it from a holder at least two feet in length, "it would be interesting to know what you require in the case of a dead human being."

"Oh, in that case I usually require an undertaker," retorted Smith dryly. "He might even be useful tonight."

"I am afraid you are not taking this case seriously, Mr. Smith," interrupted Mrs. Fanhaven. "You are pretending splendidly for our entertainment. You are an exceptional man or I should not permit it. Please go on."

"We all wear masks," retorted Smith quickly. "Few of us ever take them off. Your own mask is beautiful and almost impenetrable.

Years ago, if one believed in reincarnation, you stepped to the guillotine smelling a rose. Exposure of emotion is not done in your world in little things or in great things. Few know the difference between great and small. There is not much difference, amid infinity, between the sinking of a continent and the death of a canary."

"Ah, Gregory," said Mrs. Fanhaven, "we are fortunate in having this guest at our last dinner. If he could only prove some of his words." She turned to Smith. "Tear a mask from one of us, please."

"Your own face, madam," answered Smith, "has shown no grief over the death of your pet, and yet —"

Suddenly he reached for her hand, which was clenched, and uncurled the fingers to expose deep, biting marks of the nails upon the pink palm.

"Poor boy!" she said, glancing back toward the cage.

"I say, capital!" remarked Avondale with a supercilious smile unseen to the lady.

Mrs. Fanhaven seemed to sense some tension between the two men and glanced from one to the other.

"You know," she said, "I should like to see a contest between the two of you. What a drama it would make! I wonder which would win."

"Suppose we try?" suggested Avondale.

"By all means," returned Smith.

"And the one to tear the mask from the other," concluded Mrs. Fanhaven, "shall have any book from my late husband's library. There are some rare first editions."

"I see a *Problemata Aristotelis*," remarked Smith, strolling over to the books.

Slowly, he circled the room, apparently examining the titles, but stopping to speak occasionally, a comment upon a book or its binding. Once he brought up another topic, but without a stress that would indicate importance.

"The letter you wrote me, Mrs. Fanhaven," he said, "just reached me by the last mail this afternoon. Surely there must have been some delay in posting it."

"Gregory was going to post it," replied Mrs. Fanhaven, "but he couldn't tear himself away from a French novel, and I sent a servant to post it at the last minute."

"I am sure Mr. Avondale was quite upset when he discovered his neglect," suggested Smith.

"As a matter of fact, he was," said Mrs. Fanhaven, looking at Smith in some surprise.

"Lost his mask for a moment?" queried Smith.

"Gregory!" exclaimed Mrs. Fanhaven, "Mr. Smith is under your guard. You don't seem to be fighting."

"Plenty of time after dinner," remarked Avondale indifferently. "Some hot curry will put me in a better mood for the combat."

At that moment a servant entered, and the three went down broad stairs to a dining room on the first floor. A round table, set for three, glittered with silver and cut glass.

While going down the stairs, Mrs. Fanhaven asked Avondale if he had finished packing and received a reply in the affirmative.

"Gregory is sailing tonight," she explained to Smith as they sat down. "Going abroad to study hospital methods for me."

"Yes?" said Smith, with polite inquiry in his voice.

"Hospitals are my hobby," she informed him. "I am going to build one in New York. Dreadfully expensive hobby. Almost worse than golf."

"Why do you want a hospital?" asked Smith point-blank.

"Poor people!" returned Mrs. Fanhaven with the first real emphasis that her voice had carried. "The world would be better if wealthy people stopped their sentimental singing to jailbirds and turned their attention to city hospitals."

"You know," remarked Smith coolly, "you are equally attractive with or without your mask."

"I say, capital!" interposed Avondale. "By Jove! The floor is becoming strewn with masks."

"Cousin Gregory never shows his heart," said Mrs. Fanhaven quickly. "Poor boy!"

At the word cousin Smith had glanced at Avondale a little calculatingly as though examining a specimen in a new light. He turned again to Mrs. Fanhaven with polite attention.

"Yes?" he said with conventional inquiry.

"Somebody used a mashie on his heart," she explained, "while he was playing around with a fast set in England. Would you believe it?"

"Rather not!" answered Smith with that peculiar intonation that is heard east of the Atlantic.

"Gregory, I never knew you to be so tame," said Mrs. Fanhaven, looking curiously at her cousin. "He is mimicking you. Did you hear that English 'rather not'? You couldn't have done it better yourself."

"I'll talk good American to him as soon as I have had my curry."

"Live long in India?" queried Smith.

"Went to the dogs there before he smashed up in England," said Mrs. Fanhaven in that light way that carries no weight of truth or lack of truth. "Poor boy! He reformed, and I made him heir to console him for the loss of all his wicked ways."

At the word heir Smith looked across at Avondale and smiled, but there was no answering smile from the black eyes, although they looked steadily enough into the blue-gray ones.

"It seems to me that Mr. Smith has forgotten the canary," remarked Avondale.

"Merely wearing his mask, dear boy," said Mrs. Fanhaven. "Is it not so, Mr. Smith?"

"The truth is the best mask," returned Smith. "so few wear it that it is seldom recognized when worn."

The *pièce de résistance* of the dinner was to be an Indian curry, a dish in honour of Mr. Avondale before his departure.

"The cook prepared it under Gregory's instructions," explained Mrs. Fanhaven, "but he insists upon frying the Bombay duck himself."

A chafing dish, with the blue flame of alcohol beneath it, was brought in and placed before Avondale. Beside him was set an unopened box of imported Bombay duck, that small fish that has been dried in the sand below the blazing sun of India. Crumbled by the fingers over an Indian curry, it is the last epicurean touch to that Oriental dish.

With the curry there came a lull in the conversation. Mrs. Fanhaven seemed a little tired, but watched Smith rather shrewdly while his attention appeared to be entirely focussed upon the frying of the Bombay duck.

"Just a dash of cayenne pepper," said Avondale, lifting one of the fish upon a fork.

He took a silver pepperbox from beside his plate and shook it several times over the fish. It was then that Smith knew a climax had arrived.

No servant had brought that pepperbox to the table and two minutes earlier it *had not been there*.

Gently Avondale extended the fish to Mrs. Fanhaven, who took it in her fingers and broke it over the curry upon her plate as does the experienced curry eater.

And then it was Smith's turn.

"A little cayenne pepper?" asked Avondale, taking a second fish from the chafing dish with his fork.

"I think not," replied Smith, taking the fish from the fork. "It doesn't mix evenly, and a curry that is not thoroughly mixed is ruined."

"Too bad!" said Avondale, with the imitation melancholy of a card player who still retains the winning cards in his hand. "It is really too bad, old chap."

Smith broke the fish over his curry, outwardly calm, but inwardly trembling upon the point of taking drastic action at a time that might be premature. Mrs. Fanhaven was about to commence her curry, but changed her mind to raise a glass of water to her lips. It was then that the unexpected happened. The single lamp, which stood upon the table a cast a circle of soft radiance, went out!

"By Jove!" exclaimed Avondale in the darkness. "got my foot caught in the bally cord and pulled out the floor plug."

It was only a few seconds before the light came on again, and Avondale raised his head from below the table, the pepperbox still in his hand. But was it the same pepperbox? Smith scrutinized it as best he could, but it was impossible to be sure. He picked it up carelessly after Avondale had used it. The little silver box was quite *warm*, as it might have been if it had rested in a vest pocket during the first part of dinner.

"Sorry I didn't try the pepper, after all," said Smith, musingly.

"It's not too late," returned Avondale indifferently.

"Yes," retorted Smith. "The 'duck' is broken and mixed with the curry."

"Come, Gregory," suggested Mrs. Fanhaven, "show your antagonist a little courtesy and trade plates with him."

One properly mixed curry looks very much like another properly mixed curry, and a dash of cayenne pepper is quite invisible. Avondale shrugged his shoulders with indifference and changed plates with Smith.

The dinner progressed, and the curry, being exceedingly good, was entirely eaten by all three.

After dinner, the Smith's inward surprise, Mrs. Fanhaven announced her intention of retiring almost immediately.

"You don't suppose an old woman can remain beautiful and

sit up late!" she remarked laughingly. "Gregory is driving to the boat at eleven."

She extended her hand, and this time Smith kissed it.

"Better go to the library and attend to Richard," she said, turning away. "Poor boy!"

Smith looked after Mrs. Fanhaven with so much admiration that Avondale, who was standing close beside him, was completely thrown off his guard. Both men were watching Mrs. Fanhaven while Smith's hand stole under Avondale's dinner coat and extracted from a vest pocket, a silver pepperbox.

But the astute Avondale was not easily defeated.

"A mask!" he called and, as Mrs. Fanhaven turned around: "I claim a mask, dear lady! Our guest has been stealing your silver."

Mrs. Fanhaven, very much puzzled, but with no expression of annoyance, looked at Smith, who was holding the pepperbox in plain view. For the first time he lost the air of lazy assurance that was so characteristic of him. He placed the little pepperbox in his pocket, hesitated, and walked slowly toward her.

"I'm sorry," he said simply and placed the little utensil in her hand.

"Do I win the contest?" asked Avondale, affected boredom in his voice.

For a minute Mrs. Fanhaven looked at Smith's face and into his eyes.

"Keep it as a souvenir," she said and laughed as she handed back the box. "I'll sweep up the masks in the morning and count them. Bon soir."

Smith smiled at Avondale and dropped the silver pepperbox into his side pocket.

"What it is to be the devil with women!" remarked Avondale as the two men walked up the broad stairs together in the direction of the library. "Must see to the strapping of my bags. Join you later in the library before the arrival of that very big pistol — if you have the courage to wait."

"Uh-huh," said Smith, and they parted on the landing.

Inside the library Smith immediately placed a hand in his side pocket and found that the pepperbox had vanished!

"Couldn't have picked a pocket better myself," he soliloquized and gingerly took a second pepperbox from his vest pocket. "Poor old Avondale never spotted the substitution almost under his nose."

In the top of the second pepperbox was ingeniously constructed a slide opening that would operate upon the adroit touch of a finger and that was large enough to allow something other than pepper to escape. Carefully Smith returned the utensil to his vest pocket.

Around the entire room he proceeded, examining the books and more particularly the shelves. Books and bookshelves rapidly accumulate dust and, even in a well-ordered household, a very faint trace of dust may sometimes be seen.

Close to the hanging bird cage Smith paused and stared intently at the shelf where the faintest of dust coating had been disturbed and indicated that the books had been removed. In all the library they were the only books that had been moved during the last few days. Swiftly he removed two of them and as quickly put them back. From that moment he appeared to have no more curiosity.

Aurelius Smith was noted for his laziness of manner and, after replacing the two books, he proceeded to live up to his reputation although there was no audience. The most comfortable chair in the room was dragged to the centre table and placed so that one could sit in it and look over the table to where the doors opened into the hall. Cigarettes, matches, and ash tray were arranged conveniently. Several magazines were considered, but rejected in favour of a newspaper that was opened and placed with some care upon the table in front of the chair. All the lights were switched off with the exception of the lamp on the table. After a slow survey of the room Smith stretched himself in the chair. Not satisfied, he rose and shoved the lamp to the farther side of the table so that its rays fell just short of the chair. Satisfied, he sank again into the great chair and, long legs stretched, reached for a cigarette.

An hour passed, and a servant entered.

"Will you have some refreshment, sir?"

"Who sent you?" asked Smith abruptly.

"Mr. Avondale, sir," answered the man, somewhat surprised at the question. "Mr. Avondale would like to join you in a few minutes for a whisky and soda."

"Thanks, no," said Smith, and the servant departed.

Half an hour passed, and Avondale came swiftly into the room. The white shirt of his evening clothes showed through an unbuttoned travelling coat of black, and upon his head was a cloth travelling cap. One hand was in his overcoat pocket, and he came straight to the point with vindictive abruptness.

"It seems necessary for me to kill you," he said, coming straight to the table and looking across it at Smith.

"Uh-huh," said Smith without excitement, but with the slow emphasis of coming combat. "The report of your gun and my dead body would send you to the chair. Is it worth it?"

As he spoke Smith leaned slowly forward until his right hand with the newspaper rested upon the edge of the table. His left hand poised a cigarette a little below his lips. His intent, grey-blue eyes fixed themselves upon the black eyes of his scowling adversary upon whose face no mask at all remained.

"The gun in my pocket is muffled," retorted Avondale. "There will be no report, and your body will not be found until long after I am at sea."

"You forget the little pepperbox," countered Smith. "No doubt you have examined the one you picked out of my pocket on the stairs. Do you appreciate the trick I played upon you by substituting the pepperbox that I stole from the table for the one that I took from your pocket? You dare not leave that pepperbox behind you."

"It will be easy enough to take it from your pocket after I fire," replied Avondale, leaning forward so that his right hand, buried in his coat pocket, came above the surface of the table.

"It is hidden in this room so cleverly," returned Smith very quietly, "that even you couldn't find it before your boat sailed. I telephoned the hiding place to Miss Asterley. She knows the whole case up to your last entry to this room."

Suddenly Avondale backed away from the table and took the gun from his pocket, revealing the clumsy muffler upon its barrel.

"Smith," he said, "you have me in a nasty hole, but I'll get you some day if you don't force me to do it tonight in order to make my getaway. In the meantime there is some valuable jewellery in a wall safe behind the books near the bird cage. I intend to take that jewellery with me, and if you try to stop me I'll kill you just as quickly as I stopped the noise of the bird last night."

"Poor boy!" In the doorway stood Mrs. Fanhaven. At the sound of her voice Avondale turned sharply toward the door, and instantly Smith's left hand dropped the cigarette and jerked the newspaper from before his right hand, revealing the blue-black barrel of a pistol projecting over the edge of the table.

"Drop it!" barked Smith from his chair and rose as Avondale, glancing back to him, allowed his clumsy, noiseless weapon to slip from his fingers to the floor. "I had you covered behind the newspaper from the moment you entered the room."

"Poor Gregory," said Mrs. Fanhaven. "My lawyers warned me against you the day I changed my will in your favour. They advised me to engage Aurelius Smith to investigate you, and I did — after I saw you kill my bird from the hall after being awakened by his last few notes." She paused. "Mr. Smith will see you to the boat. Goodbye, Gregory. No, I won't shake hands; my mask is not quite thick enough for that."

Late on the afternoon of the following day Smith once more sprawled in the most comfortable chair of his diggings on Fenton Street.

The doorbell sounded, and Langa Doonh brought his master an envelope that had arrived by special messenger.

"But what *was* in the mysterious pepperbox?" asked Bernice, continuing the conversation about the recent case.

"Ah!" said Smith, opening the envelope that he had just received. "Here's the answer to your question — just arrived from a chemical laboratory. 'The little box contained [reading] a dried powdered culture of Botulinus bacillus mixed with sufficient powdered cochineal to give the whole a reddish colour. Injected into food, this mixture would have no taste and no effect for several hours, but the toxin resulting from the growth of the Botulinus bacillus would produce death by paralysis of the organs of respiration in about fifteen hours.'"

"Good Heavens!" exclaimed Bernice. "Have you heard from Mrs. Fanhaven? Is she well?"

"I haven't heard from her today," answered Smith, "but the whole case hinges on the fact that, when Avondale kicked out the table light so that I could not see him change the pepper boxes, I used the darkness to change Mrs. Fanhaven's plate for mine."

"Oh!" exclaimed Bernice a little startled.

"And of course you remember," went on Smith, "that Avondale and I changed plates after the light went on again."

"I wonder —" began Bernice.

"Here it is by wireless in the paper," interrupted Smith, "Strange and sudden death of Gregory Avondale on board the outward-bound —"

This page intentionally left blank

THE CLASP OF RANK

by
S. Carleton
from *The Thrill Book*, April 1, 1919

"For murder, though it have no tongue, will speak
With most miraculous organ."
— *Hamlet*

This page intentionally left blank

My solitary job in the winter bush was over. But coming back over the high barrens to my metropolitan cabin — three miles from the dizzy centre of the "settlement" comprised of the priest's house, the Indian agent's, one trader's, and a few shacks — it struck me that it was still a far cry to spring.

The morning was bitter; so cold that the water froze in my eyes and the breath in my nostrils, though it was March and there should have been some power in the sun. But it hung, bleak and bleached, over a world of snow, where even the distant spruce belt between me and my cabin stood gray and haggard as I made the shortest cut I could toward it. Once I reached it, I was not far from home; say about twice the distance a man could throw a stone. I am particular, because I have since had reason to measure it. But I was not dreaming of that business then.

I bolted well into the shelter of my belt of spruce trees, stopped to get my pipe lit, and ducked instinctively under the nearest tree.

Something metallic and gleaming had arched in the sombre boughs above me like a falling star. Like a star, too, I had not heard it drop, or I would have sworn someone had thrown a knife at me from behind and missed. For half a breath I thought I heard the faint rasp of snowshoes running over the crusted snow of the barrens I had just left. I had seen no one there, but that said nothing, for between the cold and haste I had never looked anywhere but before my nose. I wheeled to peer through the thick spruces that shut me in like a fence, and laughed outright. For even as I turned my silly illusion had explained itself.

The knife that had sheered across my snow-dazzled eyes had been nothing but an icicle, and there was certainly no one running away, for my assailant was before me. There was a squaw crouching under the snow-clogged spruces between me and the barrens, among a mess of tree icicles fallen on the snow. I guessed she had tried to attract my attention by throwing one at me, and then changed her mind about it, for she crouched oddly motionless on her hands and knees in the ice-spattered snow, as if she did not think she could be seen. Her face was turned from me, yet all the same I recognized her.

"Why, it's Anne Labrador; Labrador's wife!" I thought, astounded. Labrador was the Indian chief in my district, but he and Anne and their two little children lived forty miles off, in a camp they never left except to look after their line of traps and their fur caches. I dropped in to see them whenever I was over their way, and took some sugar and stuff for their funny brown babies, who could just lisp my name. "Kwa, Anne," I shouted in Indian. "What was that you threw at me just now? And where's Labrador and the children?"

Anne neither moved nor answered. I might have been my fancy that she stared detachedly into the spruces in front of her as though she would have drawn my gaze after hers, but there was certainly an extraordinary stiff and bloodless look about her. For a moment I could almost have doubted that it was Anne. She wore no silver clasp of rank as a chief's wife in the blue shawl over her breast; she had not spoken; and she was not even looking at me. I made no step toward her, though she was not fifty feet off. I did not turn my head and stare where her eyes seemed to be staring, but I saw nothing, and when I glanced back again she was gone. She must have shifted as stealthily as a wolf to have vanished like that into the blue shadows beside her, and the stupid tension of wonder that had held me snapped and left me angry. It was Anne without doubt, and this was no way for her to behave.

"Stop these fool tricks!" I called out. "Come down to my cabin if you want to see me. It's too cold to hand around here." And it was, for as I strode angrily after the woman I was shivering, and I shivered even when I brought up against an impenetrable thicket of brush that showed no sign of her. As I checked, something pricked my ankle viciously, but I was too preoccupied over Anne's idiotic disappearance even to stoop and see if a jagged stick had torn my new leggings. However she had managed it in the deep snow, she was gone, with no more trail than a stone in water; though I might have persevered in looking for her tracks if I had not felt I was being evaded. I turned down the short cut that landed me at my own woodpile, and as I kicked the snow off my leggings against it I was unwarrantably upset. Anne and her husband were old friends of mine, and for her to play hide and seek with me struck me as a very poor joke. My cabin felt colder than outside when I went into it; the fire would not burn, and I had mislaid my tobacco. Altogether the day went so crooked with me that it was with no feeling of surprise that I saw Lazier, the Indian agent, walk in that afternoon on an unasked visit.

"Things seem cut in the piece today!" I thought savagely, for he was the one man in the district for whom I had no use. He had never been in my house before, and I could not see why he had come now. It was absurd to say he wanted to hear my news. I said I had been in the bush and heard no voice but my own for a month, which was strictly true. For Anne Labrador had certainly not spoken to me that morning, and in any case I had forgotten her.

"You're a lonely man, Devlin, but if there is any news they say you are sure to hear it," Lazier assented dryly. I don't know why it struck me that he had come to find out something; there was no curiosity in his face, and it might have been by accident that his eyes searched my bare room. But I was not sorry when he suddenly said he must be going, if I saw less than ever why he had seen fit to come all the way from the settlement on such a day.

I was colder than ever, and the setting sun beat up from the snow in an intolerable glitter of colour as I watched him walk away from my door. The track he left across my clearing lay dead and blue between the crusted drifts of gold and rose and crimson, and it pleased me to think it the spirit and image of the way the man trod this world.

"Well, deliver me from any dealings with him!" said I, and banged my door.

I may as well set down why I hated Lazier. He farmed his wretched Indians. They never saw half of their government allowance; he was always sniffing out their poor quarrels, and our district was getting a bad name. If a man took out a knife he was a murderer, if he borrowed an axe he was a thief, and Lazier confiscated his flour enough to catch him out on it, even if there had been any one but the settlement priest and myself who cared. He had once tried to drag me into his thief catching, and I was so angry at the memory that I forgot to throw any wood on my fire, and neither troubled to light my lamp nor to close the shutters of my window. It was with a start that I saw my fire was out, and the new moon shining in on me. I stood up to close my shutter, and saw more than the moon.

Lazier had come back, and at the sight of him I knew I had guessed right that afternoon. He had come to find out something, and when it was clear that I did not know it had returned to discover it for himself. I opened my door in a soundless, inch-wide crack, and stood waiting to tell him it was no good, that I would give no liars nor mischief brewers the run of my house, and I must have stood ten minutes before I saw he was not coming near my house, was not thinking of me at all. He was looking for something in the snow. Sometimes he went on all fours to it; then he peered among the snow-choked spruces; then prowled into my clearing again and pounced at one place and nothing in the snow. It was not a pleasant sight as he flitted in and out of the silent bush between me and the clean new moon, yet sheer curiosity kept me from shouting to know what he wanted in my clearing. But whatever it was, I thought suddenly that he must have found it, for he stood still and so unconscious of me that I heard him laugh with relief before he vanished into the bush at a round trot for the settlement. I stared after him, raging that I had missed ordering him off my place for the second time that day. It was the cold on my face through the door crack that brought me to my senses and the knowledge that I was making a fool of myself; if the man had lost anything in the afternoon he had a perfect right to come and look for it in the evening, only I did not believe he had lost anything. It swept over me with a sudden trouble, and with no earthly reason, that it was a strange track he looked for, where no feet but his or mine had passed that day! I hunted uselessly for that or anything else he might have been looking for, and ended flatly enough at my woodpile to gather bark to rekindle my forgotten fire. Going back into my dark house with the bark under my arm, I though something fell from it with a ring like metal, but it wasn't till I knelt in the heartening leap of a four-foot blaze that I turned to look, and I kept on looking.

The thing at my feet was not what Lazier had lost. The only Indian property he owned was a crooked knife with a round handle of a kind never used in our district. And on my floor lay what never would have been given to him, and even he would not have dared to take: a squaw's niskaman, or clasp of rank. They are slightly convex disks of native silver with a round hole in the middle, through which the two ends of a shawl are pushed and secured by a hinged pin the size of a two-inch nail, but flattened to the point of a dagger. Held in a woman's hand, with the pine, upright, the clasp would give a nasty wound, but I never heard of one being used a weapon. The clasp of captain's wife in an Indian tribe is perforated in a design of which the motive is a long diamond, and is pretty enough — but this was no badge of a captain's wife! It was the clasp of a chief's wife, three inches in diameter, but cut in circles and half circles; dear to the owner as her honour, and as hard to steal. More than that, it was a clasp I knew, for I had often handled it.

"Anne Labrador's!" said I. I remembered irrelevantly, and with a curious stare, how Anne's two children had been wont to finger it where it shone on her breast. "She must have lost it before it I met her this morning! But why on earth hasn't she come to look for it?"

The dull silver of the thing held my eyes where it lay on the floor. I reached for it, wondering if I could be mistaken in it, and saw on it the symbol writing Labrador himself had taught me how to read. There was only one character, in angles and uprights, that might have represented either a three-branched candlestick or a devil, if I had not known it stood for a long word that means "my soul." Anne Labrador's own hand had cut it there, and I knew the meaning she set to it. Oddly enough, it occurred to me for the first time that it was a terrible meaning. And then I grinned at my own foolishness, since, while Anne was alive, the sign writing on her clasp meant nothing at all. For the superstition is this:

To cut the symbol of your own soul on your dearest belonging is to make it possible — if you so please, or happen to have earthly business a dead body cannot finish for you — that your spirit can enter into that belonging when you die and put life into it till it can go where it chooses and work out the desire of the dead. Anne Labrador believed it, for she had often told me so. She never let her silver clasp out of her sight, either, which made it the more unaccountable for it to have been lying on my woodpile. If she had lost it, why had she not told me when I met her in the morning? I wondered what could be wrong with the woman to make her prowl round my cabin in secret and run away when I spoke to her, but it is no use wondering where Indians are concerned, even though you know best. I put the clasp away till Anne chose to come to her senses and ask about it, and it was at that minute that the knock felt on my door.

"She's come now," I thought crossly, for I wanted to go to bed. But it was not Anne I opened the door on. It was an Indian, not a squaw, who brushed past me and stumbled over to my fire without speech or leave. I had words on my tongue till I saw the set of his mouth, and that the moccasins on his feet were frayed through. Even when he was fed he sat without speaking till I asked what he wanted of me, for he was an Indian whom I knew. "Nothing," he answered in English. "We come for the priest. Very bad news we bring. Our chief is killed."

"What chief?" I asked stupidly. "Where?"

"Labrador — over there where he camps!"

"Labrador?" Anne's husband?" I stood like a fool, thinking that it was no wonder Anne had not had the heart to speak to me that morning.

The Indian nodded, muttering: "That man who spies says his woman killed him," and I knew he meant Lazier. He rose, staggering with the words that tore out of him in the Indian tongue he had used before: "She is my sister, my sister that is younger than I, and he will hang her to a rope when he finds her. He says he saw her running from her dead, without her rank clasp that she threw away when she — she was a chief's wife no longer! He says she left her little children to the wolves that they might not weigh down her feet; he has their shawls all torn and bloody! He says if she did not kill her man why did she run? And where are the children? He says her rank clasp, that was her honour, she has thrown away into the snow!"

"Anne killed Labrador — and left the children! I don't believe it, nor the rest of the stuff about her clasp and running away." I began scornfully, and stopped, remembering Anne as she had knelt in the snow that morning without the children I had never known her to leave, Anne's rank clasp that lay in my pocket. I dared not speak of either. I turned on her brother instead. "Why do you come to me?"

"Too-ok," he returned vacantly. (The word is an expression used by an Indian when he does not know or will not say.) "I could walk no longer to the priest, and I saw your house."

My mind spun like a wheel. To the best of my belief, Anne, innocent or guilty, was hidden close by my very clearing; she had certainly left her clasp in it, for there was no other way it could have come there; but I was afraid to say so, even to her brother, till I knew the rights of the story. Neither then nor till long after did I remember the shining thing I had seen arc over my head in the spruce trees that I thought was an icicle Anne had thrown at me, though even then I should have known better. Two other thoughts held me in a cold grip — the little bloodstained shawls of two children left to the wolves and the unostentatious return of Lazier to quarter my clearing in the moonlight for a track. I turned on Anne's brother again: "Why does Lazier say Anne killed her husband? Has he found her?"

"He looks for her; she is as good as found." He stared before him dully. "I ran a long way round that he might not know I came to the priest for help. But what can the priest do?"

"Go and see!" But it stuck in my throat, remembering Anne's silence as she crouched alone in the snow. What could any man do, if what that silence said were true? I stopped the Indian as he turned.

"Tell me all you know first!"

"All I saw," he changed the verb to a literal one, "was Labrador lying dead, very lonely in his house. And the little children's shawls the man found. My sister no one saw."

"No one will!" But I did not think it. I had seen her already, and Lazier had ways of his own in the district. He had used them to get Michail Paul hanged when we all knew he was crazy, and the sheriff was his led captain.

II

I put Anne's brother out on his way to the priest, and came back with my mind spinning harder than ever. If Anne had not thrown away her clasp, which was equivalent to throwing away her rank and her people, why was it in my pocket? Unless she had killed her man, why had she crouched and run from me? And, above all, in God's name, what had happened to her little children? But there I knew in my soul furiously that Lazier was a liar. Anne was a passionately good mother; she would have fought to the death before she left her children to the wolves. That was some explanation of that, somewhere, though all the rest was beyond me. But what was not beyond me was that it was a killing night for a woman to be out who dared not light a fire, and that even if she had killed Labrador my house could shelter her. It had sheltered worse. But though I scoured the night till my blood chilled in me I could not find Anne.

There was no sense in tearing out to her camp to look for her children; the whole settlement would be doing that. And Lazier told me so when he came in for an insolent half hour next morning, carrying a baby's torn shawl that turned my stomach. I did not throw him out of my house for the sole reason that while he was in it he could not be hunting my spruces for Anne. But I was furiously certain he had wormed out that her brother had been to me before he went to the priest, and had come up on the chance that I would let out what the priest would hide. I expected Anne to be caught any minute, somewhere close to my clearing, and Lazier to haul me into witnessing against her; how I did not know, but somehow. Only those were not all the reasons that made me steal out of my shack the second Lazier had left me for the village and the sheriff and make a swift and devious departure into the tenantless barrens north of me. The others were an errand of my own, though I knew it was more like a crazy obsession, and a black certainty that sooner or later Lazier would find Anne's clasp in my possession. It was in my pocket all the time he talked to me that morning, and I knew what he would have thought if he had guessed it, which only luck had stopped. Therefore, before I crept out of my own house like a thief and before dinner I hid the clasp.

Ten miles south of the camp where Labrador had been killed lay a district where he had always run a line of traps and kept a fur cache or two. A huge green meteorite marked its boundary, and with that crazy obsession of my own in my head I snowshoed all day to get there, and at sunset saw my landmark of the green boulder shining like an emerald under the rose-coloured sky.

"Praise be!" said I, for I had enough walking; but it was something else, too. My real errand to the place was nothing on earth but a hunt for Anne's children who without rhyme or reason were in my head day and night with their little brown fingers that had burrowed in my pockets for sugar and their friendly, confident eyes. I knew they had been killed by the wolves and that it was useless to look for them, yet something inside me said passionately that I had to look for them, and that if there were any chance of finding them alive it was out here — by the green rock.

I had a perfectly unfounded certainty that Anne had taken her children with her when she fled, that even her iron strength would be exhausted by carrying and dragging the two little things till she must have stopped here by the green rock, and nowhere else, to make a fire and feed them, and more, hide them in some makeshift camp where they might still be alive. And when I say all that was a crazy obsession it was, for my own eyes had seen Lazier carrying the babies' torn and bloodstained shawls that were all the wolves had left. But crazy or not, I was so set on the thing that I was certain of seeing Anne's camp, built against the other side of the rock, with Anne's children inside it, waiting for me by the dead ashes of her camp fire.

I rounded the green boulder, and checked with shock. There was no camp; there were no children. But the thing that really downed me was that I saw just the dead camp-fire ashes I had expected, only they had not been Anne's, but a white man's! The wide pile of half-burned wood said that; and Indian makes as small a pile as he can. Some stray trapper had been here not two days ago, but Anne — Anne had never been here, never made any camp, and the story the children's shawls had told was true.

I felt like a flat fool, but I felt sick, too. I was hurrying to blot out the deadly unexpectedness of those ashes with my own fire when I saw something shining in their blackness. I sweated as I looked at it, as a horse breaks out in the stable. Anne Labrador's clasp lay by that dead fire, and I had left that clasp safely stowed in my own house!

I explained the thing to myself slowly and out loud, because I was ashamed to feel as I did about it.

"You must have put something else in the hole at the back of the chimney! This has been in your pocket all the time and dropped out as you stooped to make your fire. Or else it's some other squaw's clasp that has been lost here!"

But I stammered on the lie. There was no other clasp of a

chief's wife among the Indians, and I knew well that I was this one I had carried in from my wood pile and hidden later from Lazier. I had no desire to touch the thing, but in spite of myself I looked for the three-branched candlestick on the back of it that meant the soul of Anne Labrador. It was there! And it shone too blood red in my new firelight for a thing I had left hidden at home. The incredible thought that shook me was that if Anne, dead, could send her soul into the thing, Anne, alive, might also be able to make it sentient, intelligent; that it had got out of the hole in my chimney to follow me like a hunting dog; and that the quest it hounded me on was the search for Anne's children! I had about given that up, and I had no mind to be goaded to it afresh by superstition or coincidence. I shut my eyes and pitched the clasp away from me into the spruce trees in front of my fire and the green rock. And I breathed easier when it was gone.

But the thing in my head was not so easily switched off. Though I made a scratch camp for myself, I could not rest.

All night long, I dreamed of those two Indian children, dreamed till I woke myself, certain I heard them crying. I knew it was nonsense and that there was nothing for miles but the silence of bitter cold, yet with the first gleam of daylight, I started to tramp onward again in my fool's quest for them. Anne might have made a map in some other place and left them in it, though it was not a likely expenditure of time for a woman who was fleeing for her life. But tramp as I might I could find no Indian camp nor a sign of one, and suddenly in the middle of the morning, I jerked up where I toiled through thickets and behind boulders. There again, in the snow at my feet, was the silver clasp!

In the sunlight I was ashamed of my last night's nonsense about it. But all the same I could not see how I had thrown it miles away from those dead ashes under my fire. I wondered if Anne could possibly have managed to rummage the thing out of my house after I left, and have followed me in hopes of help; afraid to call to me, but dropping the clasp to show me she was near at hand, and picking it up when I threw it away, or, for all I knew, flung it at her, for the spruces were thick. And suddenly I realized my thoughts were once more the thoughts of a fool. Anne had no share in the business; it was my own hand that had pitched the clasp where it lay. All my tramping of the morning had been merely a circle back to the place where I had slept. The spruces round me were the spruces I had camped in front of the night before; I could see the green meteorite gleam through them as I stared.

It was stupidity fit for a man who had never seen the back country before. I was thankful no one would ever know about it. But as I was back at the green rock I would eat my dinner there, and then go home, in spite of Lazier. I had found no missing children, and never would, and I was sick of Anne and the whole business. I put her clasp in my pocket for no better reason than that it seemed wasted trouble to throw it away any more, and sat down in the lee of the rock to build a new cooking fire, and, with the match in my hand to light it, I saw paralysed. Somewhere nearing me, I heard the creak of snow under snow under snowshoes, heard men's voices.

The match burned out in my hand.

"Who's in God's world?" I wondered, and suddenly I knew. Anne must really have followed me out from my shack, and men were on Anne's trail. I peered out from behind the green rock as a man peers when he is afraid, and my mind stopped in me as a jar stops a clock. Lazier was coming toward me with the sheriff and two trappers!

III

What possessed me I don't know. Not fifty Laziers could have dragged me into the hunting of Anne, but I was in a panic. I tore her clasp out of my pocket and flung it into the spruce thicket behind me, as I had flung it before, and once more I did not look to see where it went. The action took the blood from my heart, the rigidity from my mind. I knew instantly that I had been a fool to throw away the clasp, but I dared not go for it. I turned and walked out to meet Lazier.

He stopped dead, at sight of me, with a face of the most appalling and blankest rage I ever saw. There was absolutely no expression in his eyes, and they seemed suddenly to have no pattern in the irises.

"You fool, Devlin," he swore before I could speak. "Get out of this and come home! That squaw's not here, if that's why you came. And you couldn't help her, if she was."

"I'd have a try at it," said I in a passion. "I believe it's all a pack of lies about her!" But Lazier did not see fit to answer me. He made a sharp sign to the sheriff and the trappers to stay where they were, and moved round the green rock to my unkindled fire, looking at me with those eyes. "Come home," he said under his breath and furiously. "Can't you see I came out to warn you that the sheriff's after you — that he thinks you're hiding the woman?" He swung round at a stir behind him and saw the two trappers moving toward the spruce thicket. "Sit down where you are! You don't want to go for wood; Devlin's got a fire built here that we can eat by before we go back again," he shouted, and swung round on me again. "Can't you see I came to warn you" he repeated, so low that his lips barely moved.

"Why?" No more trenchant answer came to my tongue, for over Lazier's shoulder I could see the two trappers. They were no led captains like the sheriff; they were walking over to the spruces coolly, as though Lazier had never shouted at them, only I knew it was no firewood they were after. One, or both, of them had seen the silver clasp flash as I threw it behind me, and meant to find out what I had flung away.

I knew just what they would think when they found it, but there was nothing that I could do about it. I knelt down at Lazier's feet and lit my cooking fire, but before the lowest chip had kindled, the trappers' voices sent me flying into the spruces, and the instant I stood in them I knew I had thrown the silver clasp to the right place at last. For I was looking at Anne Labrador. She was on all fours on the crusted snow, stark on her hands and knees, exactly as I thought I had seen her two days ago and thirty miles away. Even now I could not believe I had not seen her, though my intelligence said it was impossible and that she must have been dead all of two days where she crouched now. A round lump under her shawl broke the smoothness of it between her shoulders, but none of us looked to see what it was, and none of us spoke. I did not, because I could see the woman's face as I did not see it in my spruces, also the shining of silver in the snow below her breast. I was all abroad as to how I had ever flung her clasp so truly. And as I thought it, I forgot the clasp, Anne, everything.

"My soul," I yelled. "The children!" I leaped, galvanized, to what might have been the muffled whine of a dying hare.

It was close by, at my very side, that I found them, and so far my crazy obsession had been just plain common sense. Only they were in no makeshift camp, but piled over with rocks in one of Labrador's fur catches that I must have passed twice that very morning and been too big a fool to think of searching, even with a child's cry in my ears all the night before. They were hungry and pitiful enough, but alive; even almost as warm among the smelling pelts that all but filled their poor expedient of safety as when they had been packed in by their dead mother outside. All their little clothes were on them, except the torn shawls with which Lazier had sickened me, and their mother's thick blue cloth petticoat was round them both. The forlorn things wailed as they clutched me, their one familiar friend among the strange men round them. A trapper raced to my fire to boil up biscuits and hot water to feed them, the other two stood and swore — inappropriately. But the sheriff laid a sudden stolid hand on my arm, and nodded backward at Anne Labrador.

"Poor soul, poor soul!" he said, and it was the first time I ever heard kindness off his tongue. "She done her best to save them!"

"Soul!" Lazier broke in sharply. "Why do you say soul?" He had stood aloof through all the fuss about the children, and at his sneering voice the five-year-old I held opened its eyes on him and jerked in my arms.

"Keep him 'way!" it yelled. "Keep him 'way! Him hit my father — make my mother run!"

A trapper gave a flashlight glance at me. Neither of us spoke.

Lazier said contemptuously: "The child's demented!" He walked toward it from where he stood before the body of Anne Labrador, and slipped as he passed the rank clasp lying on the snow. He put out a hand to save himself, but none of us realized that it was he who had screamed out like an animal till he rolled in the snow like one, with Ann Labrador's clasp sticking fast to his palm. I saw the dagger pin of it showing through the back of his hand before he tore the thing out.

"How's that devil soul clasp here?" he screamed. "I don't see how it's here!! I threw it away after I caught her here that night, running to tell the priest I'd done for Labrador. I caught her here. After that there was no running! She knelt down!"

IV

I was knocked dead silent, though I knew a little of the babbling collapse of the nerves that comes with a wound through the very middle of a man's palm.

But the sheriff blazed out. "Lazier!" he shouted, furious. "Lazier!"

But Lazier was past shouting at. He stood staring at Anne's clasp lying where it had dropped when he tore it from his hand, a spot of concentrated white sunlight on the snow, stood staring as if he were hypnotized, and spoke as the hypnotized speak.

"She knelt down," he repeated. "She said her soul would live — she would make me fear her soul!" Her body did not matter. But I lit a fire by the green rock and stayed there till she was quiet. It was midnight when I started for home. I didn't know the children —"

I saw him wrench himself to lie, saw him stand powerless, unable to do it, his eyes still glued to the shining silver clasp at his feet.

"Anyway, she'd buried them," he said gratingly. "I found their shawls, that she'd forgotten. They got blood on them somehow, and I thought of that about the wolves. I found that clasp too, stuck on my sleeve when I was passing Devlin's, and I threw it away — on the edge of the barrens. Afterward I was afraid I'd thrown it into his clearing and he'd find it. I went there twice that day to make certain he hadn't though I never could have thrown the thing that far over his spruce trees."

No one knew that better than I did, but it was not by any will of my own that I remembered the shape I had called by the name of Anne Labrador. Yet that could not have thrown the clasp on my woodpile, where I must find it, when I failed at the bidding of its eyes! For a dazed half minute I wondered if it were true that a bit of beaten silver with the soul sign on it could take life from its dead owner and go where it pleased, if it were the clasp itself that had found its way to my woodpile. I looked up and saw Lazier's face.

"Lazier and I!" my mind flashed with cold, sane relief. "It was just Lazier and I who moved the thing from start to finish."

For, of course, it was!

Standing in my spruces that cold morning, I had really heard the drag of running feet on snowshoes over the open barrens, and I knew now it was Lazier - who had just thrown away the clasp in the metallic flash I had seen arc among my trees. And it was I myself who unwittingly carried it to my woodpile by its long pin that had pricked my ankle and stuck in my leggings till I kicked the snow off them against my stacked wood. For the rest, I put the clasp in my chimney — right enough, only once more its pin had caught in my clothing, this time in the back of my sleeve, as I withdrew my arm; and from my sleeve it had dropped on the ashes of the fire Lazier had kindled by the green rock while he waited for a woman to die. As for my finding it again this very morning it would have been a wonder if I had not, since I had merely circled back to the green rock, as I explained before. Every circumstance about the clasp was quite simple; there was nothing supernatural about any of them, and once more my eyes fell on Anne Labrador, kneeling inhumanly, stiff and bloodless, in the snow, finger for finger as I had thought I saw her kneeling in my own spruces, thirty miles from the children I had just found. The memory would have brought me up with a round turn, but in that same half second my mind came down on the truth like a hammer on a nail.

"By —" I swore aloud. "There was nothing supernatural in that, either!"

Nor was there. I suppose even a poor squaw, dying agonized for her helpless children, could think hard enough of the only man who could save them to bring her image before that man's mind. Anyway, Anne had brought hers before mine, and I knew it, though I suppose telepathic vision would have been the right term. It had taken twelve hours to get me, but it had got me. I took off my cap to the splendid soul of a dead mother, and looked away to see Lazier still talking and the sheriff holding his arm.

"Stop it, Lazier!" he shouted. "You dunno what you're saying!"

"I'm saying I was afraid of the clasp and the writing on it," Lazier returned evenly, as if he were reading out of a book. "I know it's an Indian lie that life goes into a thing you cut the soul sign on, but I was afraid of it all the same, and that Devlin had it." He spoke exactly as if I were not there. "I had to keep near him to feel safe. That was why I followed him out here. I thought —"

The dazzle off Anne's clasp made the sheriff blink. He put out an absent foot and kicked it aside into the shadow of a spruce bush. It lay there dull and dead as a slice of lead, and Lazier's speech broke off short, as if he had suddenly realized his own voice and the sense of what it said. I don't know why I stood silent. I had no pity for the man.

"You're crazy!" the sheriff burst out at him. "You're talking foolishness! Nobody killed this woman. She's just dead." He wrenched away Anne's frozen down shawl, and recoiled in a kind of electrified dumbness. The round lump under it, which had broken its smoothness between the squaw's shoulders, was the round handle of Lazier's crooked Indian knife — the one such knife in the district.

The sheriff gaped at it, missed Lazier's suddenly intelligent scowl at him, and spoke like a fool: "Why, that's yours, Lazier!"

Lazier made no answer. He looked at me, at Anne's children in my arms, at the changed, inimical faces of his two trappers, at the sheriff, then at Anne Labrador. There were six of us alive, and one dead, who knew the thing that he had done, and I saw him weigh his chances of slipping free of it. He had them; the sheriff was his satellite, the country wide. Whether he would have taken them or not I cannot say. I do say he did not mean to do the thing he did. He always carried his gun cocked, and in the side pocket of his coat. He slid his hand into his pocket now, and I guessed he was going to hand his gun over to the sheriff ostentatiously and make a play for injured innocence — and time — with me and the trappers, for he was no lightning gunman who could have shot us all up. If he had looked at us things might perhaps have been different, but his eyes were on the snow beyond him, where he stood a little turned away from us, and his hand and his gun came out of his pocket just as the wheeling sunlight pierced the spruce bush behind him and once more smote Anne Labrador's silver clasp into a burning star where the sheriff had kicked it aside. The blinding dazzle of it flashed fair into Lazier's eyes. He jerked sharply away from the stabbing white light, the hand at his side flew up, and his gun snapped off like a whip, with the muzzle jammed upward under his chin, against the soft of his throat. That was all there was to it, except that he dropped full length like a tree drops beside Anne Labrador, with his own bullet clean through his brain.

"Lazier!" yelled the sheriff. He knelt over him, incredulous in spite of everything; knelt with his eyes goggling, a led captain still. "He's shot himself," he said fatuously. "He's dead! He — it ain't true what he was telling us, is it?" He couldn't have killed Labrador and then An —" He recoiled on the name, pointing to the crouching figure that did not look as if it had ever had one. "And then her for fear she'd tell, and left little children to starve in a fur cache to cover it! And what'd he mean about the clasp and bein' afraid?"

I looked at the rank clasp, with the sign that meant the soul of Anne Labrador carved deep on it.

"I don't know," I said. But I did know that it was the clasp alone that had made Lazier betray himself with his own lips; that — accident, coincidence, or whatever you like to call it — it was also nothing other than a simple sun glint on it that had made his flung-up hand close convulsively on the trigger of his gun, and that it was by no intention of mine that I had brought it from its cache in the back of my chimney nor pitched it to the very place where Anne Labrador had died.

"Can you see what he meant 'bout bein' afraid of the clasp?" the sheriff yapped again.

I said nothing. It was not his business, nor any man's, that I was afraid of it, too. The vision of Anne Labrador over in my spruces was a simple thing, and the mere wireless of one mind in tune with another. But the thought I could not fight down — in spite of all my plain knowledge that it was just Lazier and I who had carried the clasp from the green rock and back again — was that it had been Anne's ordinary, beaten-silver tank clasp that had really done the desire of a dead mother for her lost and starving children — I left out the rest — and used me for its tool

I was thankful, of course, to have found the children. But as I turned to carry them to the nearest shelter, I had once more no desire to touch that silver clasp of a chief's wife. It was a trapper who fastened it where it belonged on the dead breast of Anne Labrador.

This page intentionally left blank

THE CRIME AT BIG TREE PORTAGE

by
H. Hesketh Prichard
from *November Joe: Detective of the Woods*. Toronto: Hodder &
Stoughton, 1913.

"November Joe" is a typical member of the long-established Anglophone
community of the Gaspé and one of the earliest of Canadian amateur
sleuths.

This page intentionally left blank

CHAPTER I

It happened that in the early autumn of 1908, I, James Quaritch, of Quebec, went down to Montreal. I was at the time much engaged in an important business transaction, which after long and complicated negotiations, appeared to be nearing a successful issue. A few days after my arrival I dined with Sir Andrew McLerrick, the celebrated nerve specialist and lecturer at McGill University, who had been for many years my friend.

On similar occasions I had usually remained for half an hour after the other guests had departed, so that when he turned from saying the last good-bye, Sir Andrew found me choosing a fresh cigar.

"I cannot call to mind, James, that I invited you to help yourself to another smoke," he said. I laughed.

"Don't mention it, Andrew; I am accustomed to your manners. All the same ..."

He watched me light up. "Make the most of it, for it will be some time before you enjoy another."

"I have felt your searching eye upon me more than once tonight. What is it?"

"My dear James," said he, "the new mining amalgamation the papers are so full of, and of which I understand that you are the leading spirit, will no doubt be a great success, yet is it really worth the sacrifice of your excellent health?"

"But I feel quite as usual."

"Quite?"

"Well, much as usual."

Upon this Sir Andrew bent his pronounced eyebrows and brilliant dark eyes upon me and put me through a catechism.

"Sleep much as usual?"

"Perhaps not," I admitted unwillingly.

"Appetite as good as usual?"

"Oh, I don't know."

"Tush, man, James! Stand up!" Thereupon he began an examination which merged into a lecture, and the lecture in due course ended in my decision to take a vacation immediately — a long vacation to be spent beyond reach of letter or telegram in the woods.

"That's right! That's right!" commented Sir Andrew. "Nothing will do you more good than to forget all these mining reports and assays in an elemental moose hunt. What do the horns of that fellow with the big bell, which you have hanging in your office, measure?"

"Fifty-nine inches."

"Then go and shoot one with a spread of sixty."

"I believe you are right," said I, for in short periods I have been able to spare from my business, I have made many hunting trips and know that there is nothing like them for change of thought. "But the worst of it is that my guide, Noel Tribonet, is laid up with rheumatism and will certainly not be fit to go with me just now. Indeed, I doubt if he will ever be much good in the woods again."

"But what if I can recommend you a new man?"

"Thanks, but I have had the trouble of training Noel already."

Once again Sir Andrew allowed his penetrating black eyes to rest upon me. Then he broke into his short rare laugh.

"I can guarantee that you will not find it necessary to train November Joe."

"November Joe?"

"Yes, do you know him?"

"Curiously enough, I do. He was with me as dishwasher when I was up with Tom Todd some years ago in Maine. He was a boy then."

"What did you think of him?"

"I hadn't much opportunity of judging. Todd kept him in camp cooking most of the time. But I do remember that once when we were on the march and were overtaken by a very bad snowstorm, Todd and the boy had a difference of opinion as to the direction we should take."

"And Joe was right?"

"He was," said I. "Todd didn't like it at all."

"Tom Todd had quite a reputation, hadn't he? Naturally he would not like being put right by a boy. Well, that must be ten years ago, and Joe's twenty-four now."

"And a good man in the woods, you say?"

"None better. The most capable in this continent, I verily believe."

I was surprised at Sir Andrew's superlatives, for he was the last man to overstate his case.

"What makes you say that?"

"A habit of speaking the truth, my dear friend. If Joe is free and can go with you, you will get your moose with the sixty-inch horns I have very little doubt."

"I am afraid there is very slight chance of his being free. You must not forget it's just the beginning of the still-hunting season."

"I know that, but I believe he was retained by the Britwells, who employed him last year, and now at the last minute Old Man Britwell has decided that he is too busy to go into camp this fall. But there may still be this difficulty. I understand that November Joe has entered into some sort of contract with the provincial police."

"With the police?" I repeated.

"Yes. He is to help them in such cases as may lie within the scope of his special experience. He is, indeed, the very last person I should like to have upon my trail had I committed a murder."

I laughed. "You think he'd run you down?"

"He is a most skilled and minute observer, and you must not forget that the specialty of a Sherlock Holmes is the every-day routine of a woodsman. Observation and deduction are part and parcel of his daily existence. He literally reads as he runs. The floor of the forest is his page. And when a crime is committed in the woods, these facts are very unfortunate."

"In what way?"

"My dear James, have you never given any consideration to the markedly different circumstances which surround the wide subject of crime and its detection, where the locality is shifted from a populous or even settled country to the loneliness of some wild region. In the midst of a city, any crime of magnitude is very frequently discovered within a few hours of its committal."

"You mean that the detectives can get after the guilty person while his trail is fresh."

"Yes, but in the woods, it is far otherwise. There Nature is the criminal's best ally. She seems to league herself with him in many ways. Often she delays the discovery of his ill-doing; she covers his deeds with her leaves and her snow; his track she washes away with her rain, and more than all she provides him with a vast area of refuge, over which she sends the appointed hours of darkness, during which he can travel fast and far. Life in the wilderness is beautiful and sweet if you will, but it has its sombre places, and they are often difficult indeed to unveil."

"All things considered, it is surprising that so many woods crimes are brought home to their perpetrators."

"There you are forgetting one very important point. As you know, my profession, that of medicine, touches, at one point, very closely upon the boundaries of criminal law, and this subject of woods crimes has always possessed a singular fascination for me. I have been present at many trials and the most dangerous witnesses that I have ever seen have been men of the November Joe type, that is, practically illiterate woodsmen. Their evidence has a quality of terrible simplicity; they give minute but unanswerable details; they hold up the candle to truth with a vengeance, and this, I think, is partly due to the fact that their minds are unclouded by any atmosphere of make-believe; they have never read any sensational novels; all their experiences are at first-hand; they bring forward naked facts with sledge-hammer results."

I had listened to Sir Andrew with interest, for I knew that his precise and accurate mind was not easily influenced to the expression of a definite opinion.

"For some years," he continued, "I have studied this subject, and there is nothing that I would personally like to do better than to have the opportunity of watching November Joe at work. Where a town-bred man would see nothing but a series of blurred footsteps in the morning dew, an ordinary dweller in the woods could learn something from them, but November Joe can often reconstruct the man who made them, sometimes in a manner and with an exactitude that has struck me as little short of marvellous."

"I see he has interested you," said I, half smiling.

"I confess he has. Looked at from a scientific standpoint, I consider him the perfect product of his environment. I repeat there are few things I would enjoy more than to watch November using his experience and his supernormal senses in the unravelling of some crime of the woods."

I threw the stump of my cigar into the fire. "You have persuaded me," I said, "I will try to make a start by the end of the week. Where is Joe to be found?"

"As to that, I believe you might get into touch with him at Harding's Farm, Silent Water, Beauce."

"I'll write to him."

"Not much use. He only calls for letters when he feels inclined."

"Then I'll cable."

"He lives twenty-seven miles from the nearest office."

"Still they might send it on to him."

"Perhaps, but it is a lonely part of the country, and messengers are likely to be scarce."

"Then I'll go to Harding's and arrange the trip by word of mouth."

"That would certainly be the best plan, and anyhow, the sooner you get into the woods, the better. Besides, you will be more likely to secure Joe by doing that, as he is inclined to be shy of strangers."

I rose and shook hands with my host.

"Remember me to Joe," said he. "I like that young man. Good-bye and good luck."

CHAPTER II

Along the borders of Beauce and Maine, between the United States and Canada, lies a land of spruce forest and of hardwood ridges. Here little farms stand on the edge of the big timber, and far beyond them, in the depths of the woodlands, lie lumber camps and the wide-flung paths of trappers and pelt hunters.

I left the cars at Silent Water and rode off at once to Harding's, the house of the Beauce farmer where I meant to put up for the night. Mrs. Harding received me genially and placed an excellent supper before me. While I was eating it a squall blew up with the fall of darkness and I was glad enough to find myself in safe shelter.

Outside the wind was swishing among the pines which enclosed the farmhouse, when, inside, the bell of the telephone, which connected us with St. George, forty miles distant, rang suddenly and incongruously, high above the clamour of the forest noises.

Mrs. Harding took up the receiver and this is what I heard:

"My husband won't be home tonight; he's gone into St. George.... No, I've no one to send . . . but how can I? There is no one here but me and the children.... Well, there's Mr. Quaritch, a sport, staying the night. No, I couldn't ask him."

I came forward.

"Why not?" I inquired.

Mrs. Harding shook her head as she stood still holding the receiver. She was a matron of distinct comeliness, and she cooked amazingly well.

"You can ask me anything," I urged.

"They want some one to carry a message to November Joe," she explained. "It's the provincial police on the phone."

"I'll go."

"Joe made me promise not to send any sports after him," she said doubtfully. "They all want him now that he's famous."

"But November Joe is rather a friend of mine. I hunted with him years ago when he lived on the Montmorency."

"Is that so?" Her face relaxed a little. "Well, perhaps ..." she conceded.

"Of course, I'll carry the message."

"It's quite a way to his place. November doesn't care about strangers; he's a solitary man. You must follow the tote-road you were on today fifteen miles, turn west at the deserted lumber-camp, cross Charley's Brook, Joe lives about two acres up the far bank." She lifted the receiver. "Shall I say you'll go?"

"By all means."

A few seconds later I was at the phone taking my instructions. It appeared that the speaker was the chief of police in Quebec, who was, of course, well known to me. I will let you have his own words.

"Very good of you, I'm sure, Mr. Quaritch. Yes, we want November Joe to be told that a man named Henry Lyon has been shot in his camp down at Big Tree Portage, on Depot River. The news came in just now, telephoned through by a lumberjack who found the body. Tell Joe, please, success means fifty dollars to him. Yes, that's all. Much obliged. Yes, the sooner he hears about it, the better. Good night."

I hung up the receiver, turned to Mrs. Harding and told her the facts. That capable woman nodded decisively.

"You won't have much time to lose, then. I'll put you up a bite to eat."

As I hastily got my things together, I began asking questions about Joe.

"So November is connected with police work now?"

Mrs. Harding answered me with another question.

"Didn't you read in the newspapers about the 'Long Island Murder'?"

I remembered the case at once; it had been a nine days' wonder of headline and comment, and now I wondered how it was that I had missed the mention of Joe's name.

"November was the man who put together that puzzle for them down in New York," Mrs. Harding went on. "Ever since they have been wanting him to work with them. They offered him a hundred dollars a month to go to New York and take on detective jobs there."

"Ah, and what had he to say to that?"

"Said he wouldn't leave the woods for a thousand."

"Well?"

"They offered him the thousand."

"With what result?"

"He started out in the night for his shack. Came in here as he passed, and told my husband he would rather be tied to a tree in the woods for the rest of his life than live on Fifth Avenue. The lumberjacks and the guides hereabouts think a lot of him. Now you'd best saddle Laura — that's the big grey mare you'll find in the near stall of the stable — and go right off. There'll be a moon when the storm blows itself out."

By the help of the lantern, I saddled Laura and stumbled away into the dark and the wind. For the chief part of the way I had to lead the mare, and the dawn was grey in the open places before I reached the deserted lumber camp, and all the time my mind was busy with memories of November. Boy though he had been when I knew him, his personality had impressed itself upon me by reason of a certain adequate quietness with which he fulfilled the duties, any and disagreeable, which bearded old Tom Todd took a delight in laying upon his young shoulders.

I remembered, too, the expression of humour and mocking tolerance which used to invade the boy's face whenever Old Tom was overtaken by one of his habitual fits of talking big. Once when Tom spoke by the camp-fire of some lake to which he desired to guide me, and of which he stated that the shores had never been trodden by white man's foot, Joe had to cover his mouth with his hand. When we were alone, Todd having departed to make some necessary repairs to the canoe, I asked Joe what he meant by laughing at his elders.

"I suppose a boy's foot ain't a man's anyways," remarked Joe innocently, and more he would not say.

In fact, it was with such memories as these that I amused myself as I tramped forward over the rough paths. And now Joe was grown up into a man who had been heard of, not only within the little ring of miles that composed his home district, but a little also out in the great world beyond.

The sun was showing over the tree tops when I drew rein by the door of the shack and at the same moment came in view of the slim but powerful figure of a young man, who was busy rolling some gear into a pack. He raised himself and, just as I was about to speak, drawled out:

"My! Mr. Quaritch, you! Who'd 'a thought it?"

The young woodsman came forward with a lazy stride and gave me welcome with a curious gentleness that was one of his characteristics, but which left me in no doubt as to its geniality.

I feel that I shall never be able to describe November. Suffice it to say that the loose-knit boy I remembered had developed into one of the finest specimens of manhood that ever grew up among the balsam trees; near six feet tall, lithe and powerful, with a neck like a column, and a straight-featured face, the sheer good looks of this son of the woods were disturbing. He was clearly also not only the product but the master of his environment.

"Well, well, Mr. Quaritch, many's the time I've been thinking of the days we had with old Tom way up on the Roustik."

"They were good days, Joe, weren't they?"

"Sure, sure, they were!"

"I hope we shall have some more together."

"If it's hunting you want, I'm glad you're here, Mr. Quaritch. There's a fine buck using around by Widdeney Pond. Maybe we will get a look at him come sunset, for he most always moves out of the thick bush about dark." Then humour lit a spark in his splendid grey eyes as he looked up at me. "But we'll have a cup o' tea first."

November Joe's (by the way, I ought to mention that his birth in the month of November had given him his name), as I say, November Joe's weakness for tea had in the old days been a target upon which I had often exercised my faculty for irony and banter. The weakness was evidently still alive. I smiled; perhaps it was a relief to find a weak point in this alarmingly adequate young man.

"I had hoped to have a hunt with you, November," said I. "Indeed, that is what I came for, and there's nothing I'd like better than to try for your red deer buck tonight, but while I was at Harding's there was a ring-up on the phone, and the provincial police sent through a message for you. It appears that a man named Henry Lyon has been shot in his camp at Big Tree Portage. A lumberman found him, and phoned the news into Quebec. The chief of police wants you to take on the case. He told me to say that success would mean fifty dollars."

"That's too bad," said Joe. "I'd sooner hunt a deer than a man any day. Makes a fellow feel less bad-like when he comes up with him. Well, Mr. Quaritch, I must be getting off, but you'll be wanting another guide. There's Charley Paul down to St. Amiel."

"Look here, November, I don't want Charley Paul or any other guide but you. The fact of the matter is that Sir Andrew McLerrick, the great doctor who was out with you last fall, has told me that I have been overdoing it and must come into the woods for rest. I've three months to put in, and from all I hear of you, you won't take three months finding out who murdered Lyon."

Joe looked grave. "I may take more than that," said he, "for maybe I'll never find out at all. But I'm right pleased, Mr. Quaritch, to hear you can stay so long. There's plenty of grub in my shack, and I daresay that I shan't be many days gone."

"How far is it to Big Tree Portage?"

"Five miles to the river and eight up it."

"I'd like to go with you."

He gave me one of his quick smiles. "Then I guess you'll have to wait for your breakfast till we are in the canoe. Turn the mare loose. She'll make Harding's by afternoon."

Joe entered the shack and came out again with one or two articles. In five minutes he had put together a tent, my sleeping things, food, ammunition, and all necessaries. The whole bundle he secured with his packing strap, lifted it, and set out through the woods.

CHAPTER III

I have sometimes wondered whether he was not irked at the prospect of my proffered companionship, and whether he did not at first intend to shake me off by obvious and primitive methods.

He has in later days assured me that neither of my suppositions was correct, but there has been a far-off look in his eyes while he denies them, which leaves me still half-doubtful.

However these things may be, it is certain that I had my work, and more than my work, cut out for me in keeping up with November, who, although he was carrying a pack while I was unloaded, travelled through the woods at an astonishing pace.

He moved from the thighs, bending a little forward. However thick the underbrush and the trees, he never once halted nor even wavered, but passed onward with neither check nor pause. Meanwhile, I blundered in his tracks until at last, when we came out on the bank of a strong and swiftly flowing river, I was fairly done, and felt that, had the journey continued much longer, I must have been forced to give in.

November threw down his pack and signed to me to remain beside it, while he walked off downstream, only to reappear with a canoe.

We were soon aboard her. Of the remainder of our journey I am sorry to say I can recall very little. The rustle of the water as it hissed against our stem and the wind in the birches and junipers on the banks soon lulled me. I was only awakened by the canoe touching the bank at Big Tree.

Big Tree Portage is a recognized camping place, situated between the great main lumber camp of Briston and Harpur and the settlement of St. Amiel, and it lies about equidistant from both. Old fire scars in the clearing showed black not more than thirty yards from the water. From the canoe we were in full sight of the scene of the tragedy.

A small shelter of boughs stood beneath the spreading branches of a large fir, the ground all about was strewn with tins and debris. On a bare space in front of the shelter, beside the charred logs of a campfire, a patch of blue caught my eye. This, as my sight grew accustomed to the light, resolved itself into the shape of a huge man. He lay upon his face, and the wind fluttered the blue blouse which he was wearing. It came upon me with a shock that I was looking at the body of Henry Lyon, the murdered man.

November, standing up in the canoe, a wood's picture in his buckskin shirt and jeans, surveyed the scene in silence, then pushed off again and paddled up and down, staring at the bank. After a bit he put in and waded ashore.

In obedience to a sign, I stayed in the canoe, from which I watched the movements of my companion. First, he went to the body and examined it with minute care; next, he disappeared within the shelter, came out, and stood for a minute staring towards the river; finally, he called to me to come ashore.

I had seen November turn the body over, and as I came up I was aware of a great ginger-bearded face, horribly pale, confronting the sky. It was easy to see how the man had died, for the bullet had torn a hole at the base of the neck. The ground beside him was scored up as if by some small sharp instruments.

The idea occurred to me that I would try my hand at detection. I went into the shelter. There I found a blanket, two freshly flayed bear skins, and a pack, which lay open. I came out again and carefully examined the ground in all directions. Suddenly looking up, I saw November Joe watching me with a kind of grim and covert amusement.

"What are you looking for?" said he.

"The tracks of the murderer."

"You won't find them."

"Why?"

"He didn't make none."

I pointed out the spot where the ground was torn.

"The lumberman that found him — spiked boots," said November.

"How do you know he was not the murderer?"

"He didn't get here till Lyon had been dead for hours. Compare his tracks with Lyon's ... much fresher. No, Mr. Sport, that cock won't fight."

"Then, as you seem to know so much, tell me what you *do* know."

"I know that Lyon reached here in the afternoon of the day before yesterday. He'd been visiting his traps upstream. He hadn't been here more'n a few minutes, and was lighting his pipe in the shelter there, when he hears a voice hail him. He comes out and sees a man in a canoe shoved into the bank. That man shot him dead and cleared off — without leaving a trace."

"How can you be sure of all this?" I asked, for not one of these things had occurred to my mind.

"Because I found a pipe of tobacco not rightly lit, but just charred on top, beside Lyon's body, and a new-used match in this shack. The man that killed him come downstream and surprised him."

"How can you tell he came downstream?"

"Because, if he'd come upstream, Lyon would 'a seen him from the shack," said November with admirable patience.

"You say the shot was fired from a canoe?"

"The river's too wide to shoot across; and, anyway, there's the mark of where the canoe rested agin the bank. No, this is the work of a right smart woodsman, and he's not left me one clue as to who he is. But I'm not through with him, mister. Such men as he needs catching.... Let's boil the kettle.

* * * * *

We laid the dead man inside the shack, and then, coming out once more into the sunlight, sat down beside a fire, which we built among the stones on the bank of the river. Here November made tea in true woods fashion, drawing all the strength and bitterness from the leaves by boiling them. I was wondering what he would do next, for it appeared to me that our chance of catching the murderer was infinitesimal, since he had left no clue save the mark on the bank where his canoe had rested among the reeds while he fired his deadly bullet. I put my thoughts into words.

"You're right," said November. "When a chap who's used to the woods life takes to crime, he's harder to lay hands on than a lynx in an alder patch."

"There is one thing which I don't understand," said I. "Why did not the murderer sink Lyon's body in the water? It would have been well hidden there."

The young woodsman pointed to the river, which foamed in low rapids about dark heads of rock.

"He couldn't trust her; the current's sharp, and would put the dead man ashore as like as not," he replied. "And, if he'd landed to carry it down to his canoe, he'd have left tracks. No, he's done his work to rights from his point of view."

I saw the force of the argument, and nodded.

"And more'n that, there's few people," he went on, "travel up and down this river. Lyon might 'a laid in that clearing till he was a skeleton, but for the chance of that lumberjack happening along."

"Then which way do you think the murderer has fled?"

"Can't say," said he, "and, anyhow, he's maybe eighty miles away by this time."

"Will you try and follow him?"

"No, not yet. I must find out something about him first. But, look here, mister, there's one fact you haven't given much weight to. This shooting was premeditated. The murderer *knew* that Lyon would camp here. The chances are a hundred to one against their having met by accident. The chap that killed him followed him downstream. Now, suppose I can find Lyon's last camp, I may learn something more. It can't be very far off, for he had a tidy-sized pack to carry, besides those green skins, which loaded him a bit.... And, anyway, it's my only chance."

So we set out upon our walk. November soon picked up Lyon's trail, leading from Big Tree Portage to a disused tote road, which again led us due west between the aisles of the forest. From midday on through the whole of the afternoon we travelled. Squirrels chattered and hissed at us from the spruces, hardwood partridges drummed in the clearings, and once a red-deer buck bounded across our path with its white flag waving and dipping as it was swallowed up in the sun-speckled orange and red of the woods.

Lyon's trail was, fortunately, easy to follow, and it was only where, at long intervals, paths from the north or south broke into the main logging road that November had reason to pause. But one by one we passed these by, until at last the tracks we were following shot away among the trees, and after a mile of deadfalls and moss debouched into a little clearing beside a backwater grown round with high yellow grass, and covered over the larger part of its surface with lily-pads.

The trail, after leading along the margin of this water struck back to a higher reach of the same river that ran by Big Tree Portage, and then we were at once on the site of the deserted camp.

The very first thing my eye lit upon caused me to cry out in excitement, for side by side were two beds of balsam branches, which had evidently been placed under the shelter of the same tent cover. November then, was right. Lyon *had* camped with someone on the night before he died.

I called out to him. His quiet patience and an attitude as if rather detached from events fell away from him like a cloak, and with almost uncanny swiftness he was making his examination of the camp.

I entirely believe that he was unconscious of my presence, so concentrated was he on his work as I followed him from spot to spot with an interest and excitement that no form of big-game shooting has ever given me. Now, man was the quarry and, as it seemed, a man more dangerous than any beast. But I was destined to disappointment, for, as far as I could see, Joe discovered neither clues nor anything unusual.

To begin with, he took up and sifted through the layers of balsam boughs which had composed the beds, but apparently made no find. From them he turned quickly to kneel down by the ashy remains of the fire, and to examine the charred logs one by one. After that he followed a well-marked trail that led away from the lake to a small marsh in the farthest part of which masts of dead timber were standing in great profusion. Nearer at hand a number of stumps showed where the campers had chopped the wood for their fire.

After looking closely at these stumps, November went swiftly back to the camp and spent the next ten minutes in following the tracks which led in all directions. Then once more he came back to the fire and methodically lifted off one charred stick after another. At the time I could not imagine why he did this, but, when I understood it, the reason was as simple and obvious as was that of his every action when once it was explained.

Before men leave a camp they seem instinctively to throw such trifles as they do not require or wish to carry on with them in the fire, which is generally expiring, for a first axiom of the true camper in the woods is never to leave his fire alight behind him, in case of a chance ember starting a forest conflagration.

In this case November had taken off nearly every bit of wood before I heard him utter a smothered exclamation as he held up a piece of stick.

I took it into my own hands and looked it over. It was charred, but I saw that one end had been split and the other end sharpened.

"What in the world is it?" I asked, puzzled.

November smiled. "Just evidence," he answered.

I was glad he had at last found something to go upon, for, so far, the camp had appeared to produce parsimoniously little that was suggestive. Nevertheless, I did not see how this little bit of spruce, crudely fashioned and split, as it was, would lead us very far.

November spent another few minutes in looking everything over a second time, then he took his axe and split a couple of logs and lit the fire. Over it he hung his inevitable kettle and boiled up the leaves of our morning brew with a liberal handful freshly added. Soon the steam was hissing up into the quiet air.

"Well," I said, as he touched the end of a burning ember to his pipe, "has this camp helped you?"

"Some," said November. "And you?"

He put the question quite seriously, though I suspect not without some inward irony.

"I can see that two men slept here under one tent cover, that they cut the wood for their fire in that marsh we visited, and that they were here for a day, perhaps two."

"One was here for three days, the other one night," corrected November.

"How can you tell that?"

November pointed to the ground at the far end side of the fire.

"To begin with, number one had his camp pitched over there," said he; then, seeing my look of perplexity, he added pityingly: "We've a westerly wind these last two days, but before that the wind was east, and he camped the first night with his back to it. And in the new camp one bed o' boughs is fresher than the other."

The thing seemed so absurdly obvious that I was nettled.

"I suppose there are other indications I haven't noticed," I said.

"There might be some you haven't mentioned," he answered warily.

"What are they?"

"That the man who killed Lyon is thick-set and very strong; that he has been a good while in the woods without having gone to a settlement; that he owns a blunt hatchet such as we woods chaps call 'tomahawk, number three'; that he killed a moose last week arriving the following evening; that about half a mile short of the settlement, he landed and that he can read; that he spent the night before the murder in great trouble of mind, and that likely he was a religious kind of chap."

As November reeled off these details in his quiet, low-keyed voice, I stared at him in amazement.

"But, how can you have found out all that?" I said at last. "If it's correct it's wonderful!"

"I'll tell you, if you still want to hear, when I've got my man — if ever I do get him. One thing more is sure, he is a chap who knew Lyon well. The rest of the job lies in the settlement of St. Amiel, where Lyon lived."

We walked back to Big Tree Portage, and from there ran down in the canoe to St. Amiel, set up our camp. Afterwards we went on. I had never before visited the place, and I found it to be a little colony of scattered houses, straggling beside the river. It possessed two stores and one of the smallest churches I have ever seen.

"You can help me here if you will," said November as we paused before the larger of the stores.

"Of course I will. How?"

"By letting 'em think you've engaged me as your guide and we've come in to St. Amiel to buy some grub and gear we've run short of."

"All right." And with this arrangement we entered the store.

I will not make any attempt to describe by what roundabout courses of talk November learned all the news of desolate little St. Amiel and of the surrounding countryside. Had I not known exactly what he wanted, I should never have dreamed that he was seeking information. He played the desultory uninterested listener to perfection. The provincial police had evidently found means to close the mouth of the lumberjack for the time, at least, as no hint of Lyon's death had yet drifted back to his native place.

Little by little it came out that only five men were absent from the settlement. Two of these, Fitz and Baxter Gurd, were brothers who had gone on an extended trapping expedition. The other absentees were Highamson, Lyon's father-in-law; Thomas Miller, a professional guide and hunter; and, lastly, Henry Lyon himself, who had gone up-river to visit his traps, starting on the previous Friday. The other men had all been away three weeks or more, and all had started in canoes, except Lyon, who, having sold his, went on foot.

Next, by imperceptible degrees, the talk slid round to the subject of Lyon's wife. They had been married four years and had no child. She had been the belle of St. Amiel, and there had been no small competition for her hand. Of the absent men, both Miller and Fitz Gurd had been her suitors, and the former and Lyon had never been on good terms since the marriage. The younger Gurd was a wild fellow, and only his brother's influence kept him straight.

So much we heard before November wrapped up our purchases and we took our leave.

No sooner were we away than I put my eager question: "What do you think of it?"

Joe shrugged his shoulders.

"Do you know any of these men?"

"All of them."

"How about the other fellow who is on bad terms with —"

November seized my arm. A man was approaching through the dusk. As he passed my companion hailed him.

"Hullo, Baxter! Didn't know you'd come back. Where you been?"

"Right up on the headwaters."

"Fitz come down with you?"

"No; stayed on the line of traps. Did you want to see him, November?"

"Yes, but it can wait. See any moose?"

"Nary one — nothing but red deer."

"Good-night."

"So long."

"That settles it," said November. "If he speaks the truth, as I believe he does, it wasn't either of the Gurds shot Lyon."

"Why not?"

"Didn't you hear him say they hadn't seen any moose? And I told you the man that shot Lyon had killed a moose quite recent. That leaves just Miller and Highamson — and it weren't Miller."

"You're sure of that?"

"Stark certain. One reason is that Miller's above six feet, and the man who camped with Lyon wasn't as tall by six inches. Another reason. You heard the storekeeper say how Miller and

Lyon wasn't on speaking terms; yet the man who shot Lyon camped with him — slep' beside him — must 'a talked to him. That weren't Miller."

His clear reasoning rang true.

"Highamson lives alone away up above Lyon's," continued November. "He'll make back home soon."

"Unless he's guilty and has fled the country," I suggested.

"He won't 'a done that. It 'ud be as good as a confession. No, he thinks he's done his work to rights and has nothing to fear. Like as not he's back home now. There's not much coming and going between these up-river places and St. Amiel, and he might easy be there and no one knew it yet down to the settlement. We'll go up tonight and make sure. But first we'll get back to camp and take a cup o' tea."

The night had become both wild and blustering before we set out for Highamson's hut, and all along the forest paths which led to it, the sleet and snow of what November called "a real mean night" beat in our faces.

As we travelled on in silence, my mind kept going over and over the events of the last two days. I had already seen enough to assure me that my companion was a very skillful detective, but the most ingenious part of his work, namely, the deductions by which he had pretended to reconstruct the personality of the criminal, had yet to be put to the test.

It was black dark, or nearly so, when at last a building loomed up in front of us, a faint light showing under the door.

"You there Highamson?" called out November.

As there was no answer, my companion pushed it open and we entered the small wooden room, where, on a single table, a lamp burned dimly. He turned it up and looked around. A pack lay on the floor unopened, and a gun leant up in a corner.

"Just got in," commented November. "Hasn't loosed up his pack yet."

He turned it over. A hatchet was thrust through the wide thongs which bound it. November drew it out.

"Put your thumb along that edge," he said. "Blunt? Yes? Yet he drove that old hatchet as deep in the wood as Lyon drove his sharp one: he's a strong man."

As he spoke he was busying himself with the pack, examining its contents with deft fingers. It held little save a few clothes, a little tea and salt, and other fragments of provisions, and a Bible. The finding of the last was, I could see, no surprise to November, though the reason why he should have suspected its presence remained hidden from me. But I had begun to realize that much was plain to him which to the ordinary man was invisible.

Having satisfied himself as to every article in the pack, he rapidly replaced them, and tied it up as he had found it, when I, glancing out of the small window, saw a light moving low among the trees, to which I called November Joe's attention.

"It's likely Highamson," he said, "coming home with a lantern. Get you into that dark corner."

I did so, while November stood in the shadow at the back of the closed door. From my position I could see the lantern slowly approaching until it flung a gleam of light through the window into the hut. The next moment the door was thrust open, and the heavy breathing of a man became audible.

It happened that at first Highamson saw neither of us, so that the first intimation that he had of our presence was November's "Hello!"

Down crashed the lantern, and its bearer started back with a quick hoarse gasp.

"Who's there?" he cried, "who —"

"Them as is sent by Hal Lyon."

Never have I seen words produce so tremendous an effect.

Highamson gave a bellow of fury, and the next instant he and November were struggling together.

I sprang to my companion's aid, and even then it was no easy task for the two of us to master the powerful old man. As we held him down I caught my first sight of his ash-grey face. His mouth grinned open, and there was a terrible intention in his staring eyes. But all changed as he recognized his visitor.

"November! November Joe!" cried he.

"Get up!" And as Highamson rose to his feet, "Whatever for did you do it?" asked November in his quiet voice. But now its quietness carried a menace.

"Do what? I didn't — I —" Highamson paused, and there was something unquestionably fine about the old man as he added: "No, I won't lie. It's true I shot Hal Lyon. And, what's more, if it was to do again, I'd do it again! It's the best deed I ever done; yes, I say that, though I know it's written in the book: 'Whoso sheddeth man's blood, by man shall his blood be shed.'"

"Why did you do it?" repeated November.

Highamson gave him a look.

"I'll tell you. I did it for my little Janey's sake. He was her husband. See here! I'll tell you why I shot Hal Lyon. Along of the first week of last month I went away back into the woods trapping muskrats. I was gone more'n the month, and the day I come back I did as I did tonight, as I always do first thing when I gets in — I went over to see Janey. Hal Lyon weren't there; if he had been, I shouldn't never 'a needed to travel so far to get even with him. But that's neither here nor there. He'd gone to his bear traps above Big Tree; but the night before he left he'd got in one of his quarrels with my Janey. Hit her — he did — there was one tooth gone where his — fist fell."

Never have I seen such fury as burned in the old man's eyes as he groaned out the last words.

"Janey, that had the prettiest face for fifty miles around. She tried to hide it from me — she didn't want me to know — but there was her poor face all swole, and black and blue, and the gap among her white teeth. Bit by bit it all came out. It weren't the first time Lyon'd took his hands to her, no, nor the third, nor the fourth. There on the spot, as I looked at her, I made up my mind I'd go after him, and I'd make him promise me, aye, swear to me, on the Holy Book, never to lay hand on her again. If he wouldn't swear I'd put him where his hands couldn't reach her. I found him camped away up alongside a backwater near his traps and I told him I'd seen Janey and that he must swear.... He wouldn't! He said he'd learn her to tell on him, he'd smash her in the mouth again. Then he lay down and slep'. I wonder now he weren't afraid of me, but I suppose that was along of me being a quiet, God-fearing chap. . . Hour by hour I lay awake, and then I couldn't stand it no more, and I got up and pulled a bit of candle I had from my pack, fixed up a candlestick and looked in my Bible for guidance. And the words I lit on were: "Thou shalt break them with a rod if iron." That was the gun clear enough.... Then I blew out the light, and I think I slep', for I dreamed.

"Next morning Lyon was up early. He had two or three green skins that he'd took off the day before, and he said he was going straight home to smash Janey. I lay there and I said nothing, black nor white. His judgement was set. I knew he couldn't make all the distance in one day, and I was pretty sure he'd camp at Big Tree. I arrived there just after him, as I could travel faster by canoe than him walking, and so kep' near him all day. It was nigh sunset, and I bent down under the bank so he couldn't see me. He went into the old shack. I called out his name. I heard him cursing at my voice, and when he showed his face I shot him dead. I never landed. I never left no tracks, I thought I was safe, sure. You've took me; yet only for Janey's sake I wouldn't care. I did right, but she won't like them to say her father's a murderer.... That's all."

November sat on the edge of the table. His handsome face was grave. Nothing more was said for a good while. Then Highamson stood up.

"I'm ready, November, but you'll let me see Janey again before you give me over to the police?"

November looked him in the eyes.

"Expect you'll see a good deal of Janey yet. She'll be lonesome over there now that her brute husband's gone. She'll want you to live with her," he said.

"D'ye mean ..."

November nodded. "If the police can catch you for themselves, let 'em. And you'd lessen the chance of that a wonderful deal if you was to burn them moose-shank moccasins you're wearing. When did you kill your moose?"

"Tuesday's a week. And my moccasins was wore out, so I fixed 'em up woods fashion."

"I know. The hair on them is slipping. I found some of it in your tracks in the camp, away above Big Tree. That's how I knew you'd killed a moose. I found your candlestick too. Here it is." He took from his pocket the little piece of spruce stick, which had puzzled me so much, and turned towards me.

"This end's sharp to stick into the earth, that end's slit and you fix the candle in it with a bit o' birch bark. Now it can go into the stove along o' the moccasins": he opened the stove door and thrust in the articles.

"Only three know your secret, Highamson, and if I was you I wouldn't make it four, not even by adding a woman to it."

Highamson held out his hand.

"You always was a white man, Nov.," said he.

Hours later, as we sat drinking a final cup of tea at the camp fire, I said:

"After you examined Lyon's upper camp, you told me seven

things about the murderer. You've explained how you knew them, all but three."

"What are the three?"

"First, how did you know that Highamson had been a long time in the woods without visiting a settlement?"

"His moccasins was wore out and patched with raw moose-hide. The tracks of them was plain," replied November.

I nodded. "And how could you tell that he was religious and spent the night in great trouble of mind?"

November paused in filling his pipe. "He couldn't sleep," said he, "and so he got up and cut that candle-stick. What'd he want to light a candle for but to read by? And why should he want to read in the middle of the night if he was not in trouble? And if he was in trouble, what book would he want to read? Besides, not one trapper in a hundred carries any book but the Bible."

"I see. But how did you know it was in the middle of the night?"

"Did you notice where he cut his candlestick?"

"No," I said.

"I did, and he made two false cuts where his knife slipped in the dark. You're wonderful at questions."

"And you at answers."

November stirred the embers under the kettle, and the firelight lit up his fine face as he turned with a yawn.

"My!" said he, "but I'm glad Highamson had his reasons. I'd 'a hated to think of that old man shut in where he couldn't see the sun rise. Wouldn't you?"

THE EYES OF SEBASTIEN

by
Alan Sullivan
from *Under the Northern Lights*. Toronto: J.M. Dent, 1926.

Canada has in its supernatural lexicon two werewolves: the Wendigo of Algonkian legend, and the *loup garou* of French-Canadian folklore. Sullivan's classic tale is an exploration of the latter.

This page intentionally left blank

This is a tale of the big timber that grows in league-long patches where the headwaters of the Saguenay find their birth amongst tumbled foothills of the Laurentian range. Thence flows the Saguenay, a chill and formidable stream, gathering volume as it moves southward with countless tributaries from unknown lakes and moose-trampled marshes, loitering on its way through stretches of cedar-bordered solitude, flinging itself headlong over cataracts where the tawny water rages thunderously day and night, ever more deep, forbidding and austere, till at last it merges majestically with the great St. Lawrence, the mother of many rivers, and spends itself between the thousand-foot crags of capes Trinity and Eternity.

All along the Saguenay it is a French country, as French as when two hundred years ago the peasants of Brittany and Normandy first fared northward into the unexplored wilderness. Amid the big timber and beside unnamed waters they raised their log-hewn walls, with the mud-chinked joints, the tiny deep-set windows and the massive roofs that must bear the weight of winter snows. Out of the forest they carved their farms, planting grain between the unconquerable roots, drawing sustenance from wood and stream, beating off marauding Indians, gathering in the long winter evenings round pine-heaped hearths, utterly alone save when in summer the yellow bows of a canoe glided round a point, and a missionary Jesuit Father landed from Quebec; or when in winter the man of God tramped, solitary, through endless miles of big timber on his errand of mercy and peace.

But always there was talk of France, with lingering, poignant pictures of the land they had left, of the red roofs of Quiberon that look across the bay at Croise and the cobbled streets of Rennes that lead to the swift waters of the Vilaine.

In one of the patches of timber on Lac St. Luc there is a lumber camp, a nest of long buildings, ten feet high, that occupy a roughly cleared space close to the water's edge. From the camp there radiates a maze of winter roads traversed by a hundred lumberjacks in gaudy woollen capotes, with axes and saws over their shoulders, and down these roads, which all slope gently to the lake, great logs are drawn, to be dumped, rumbling, on the ice. All through the day one can hear, near and far, the crash of big timber toppling earthward, the creak of straining harness, the crack of whips, the stroke of axes and the whine of distant saws. At night there is talk beside great cast-iron stoves stuffed with fuel, much smoke, the drone of winter winds and the plaintive hoot of the great white owl.

It fell on a day when the sun shone bright and the snow was like a sparkling blanket, that a man emerged from the Saguenay trail and struck across Lac St. Luc. He walked with a long, easy swing, bending a little forward beneath the weight of his pack. Threading his way between the piles of logs, he halted at the door of the main building, twisted his feet free of snowshoes and entered.

"Holla!" he said with a smile. "I have again arrived."

The cook looked round, and straightway forgot his cooking, for the newcomer was none other than Antoine Carnot the peddler — the bringer of news — the teller of tales — the confidential go-between in the wilderness — the human link with the outside world. Antoine was all of these, and more. A bit of a doctor, a bit more of a lawyer, a shrewd trader, and withal possessed of unfailing humour and a heart of gold. No wonder that Pierre Colange forgot his cooking and hurried forward, hands outstretched.

"Ten thousand welcomes, *mon vieux*. No, you shall not talk till you have eaten. Behold, a partridge which was for the boss, but eat and say nothing. The wind makes a chill in the stomach, but you have an hour before the men come in. Fill thyself, and say nothing till afterwards."

Antoine nodded and obeyed, while Pierre watched him admiringly. Then there was news, much news from a dozen villages, while the pack was unrolled and its contents spread on a table in the corner. Knives and neckties, shirts and razors and mouth organs, jimcrackers and cheap jewellery, studs and celluloid collars — the result of Antoine's annual trip to Quebec. Presently his wares were displayed to his satisfaction, and he sent Pierre a swift glance.

"Jean Deslormes, he is still here?"

Pierre nodded. "He makes good money, forty dollars a month — and spends nothing save for tobacco."

"I was at Villeneuve this day two weeks ago," said Antoine thoughtfully, "and saw the girl Marie Fisette. They are betrothed."

Pierre laughed at this. "Does not the whole camp know it, and how many times has Jean not told us! Every morning he goes along the road making verses to that girl with his mouth. It is well that he cannot write — but perhaps I do not understand such things. I made no verses to my Henriette."

Antoine looked a little grave. "Sebastien was also at Villeneuve, and full of anger when he heard of the betrothal. Marie told me that he said strange and threatening things, that she should never marry Jean. Then he barked something like a wolf, and she did not see him again."

"Loup Garou!" whispered Pierre under his breath.

It was a word of awe through the outlying French country. The story of the Loup Garou, that strange and malign combination of man and wolf, had come across with them from the hills of Brittany. The belief still held north of the Laurentians. It was always an old dog wolf, tenanted by some evil and human spirit, endowed with wild powers of murder and revenge, a lean grey beast that patrolled the winter hills and sent his savage note drifting down into solitary villages where simple folk gathered closer round the fire and glanced apprehensively at the window fastenings. Sometimes it was a man who took the form of a wolf to serve his dread purpose, and became again human when his deadly part was played.

This had been whispered of Sebastien behind his back. Where

the man came from, none knew, only that calamity came with him. He was small, dark, and very active, with hollow cheeks and burning eyes, and moved about through the French country, seldom doing any work, but living apparently without effort. He was disliked and feared, but the folk made no protest — at least to Sebastien. There was the case of Georges Famieux who threw Sebastien out of his barn one evening, and next morning found his prize cow with her throat torn. One remembered that sort of thing in a district where cows were scarce. So now the good Antoine pushed out his lips and nodded gravely.

"Yes," he said thoughtfully. "It can be nothing else."

A little silence fell in the cook's camp, and both men had a vision of Marie Fisette of the parish of Villeneuve, Marie the prettiest girl north of Cape Trinity, with her flaxen hair and white skin like milk and a smile that was remembered and treasured enviously in every lumber camp on the Saguenay. They said that she chose Jean Deslormes when she saw him driving logs through the chute at Les Arables. And what Jean did then ought to be enough for any girl.

"They will be married this summer — yes?" asked Pierre.

And just at this moment the door opened without sound, and Sebastien himself strolled in. He rubbed his long hands to set the blood going, glanced shrewdly at the two men and stared meaningfully toward the heaped platters on the stove. Pierre gave him food, this being the law of the wilderness, while Antoine began to rearrange his stock. Both were a little breathless. Presently Sebastien pushed away his plate.

"Without doubt, Pierre, you are the best cook in the Saguenay camps. I will tell them so in Villeneuve." He lit his pipe and began to smoke contentedly.

"You go then to Villeneuve?" hazarded Antoine.

"Yes, I start at once, this very day."

"By the Saguenay trail?"

Sebastien sent him an inscrutable smile. "My trail is my own, Antoine"; then, meaningfully, "let him follow who can."

"It is ninety miles to Villeneuve as the goose flies. What takes you there in midwinter?"

"The thing that takes all men to all places no matter what the season. The face of a woman."

Pierre lifted a kettle from the stove, and the lid rattled. "Is it then that Sebastien marries at his age?"

"What is age to the man who desires? In five days I shall have what has been desired by many."

He announced this in a voice that lifted as he spoke, and surveyed the others with burning, insolent eyes as though daring them to protest. There was in his manner something suggesting that he had at his disposal powers of which they knew nothing. He leaned a little forward, every line of his sinewy body resembling an animal crouched to spring, and there was but one animal in the minds of the others. He was known to travel swiftly, and always alone, but no man had ever found his tracks. And though he could not marry till after he had been in Villeneuve for at least three days, he now stated he would marry in five. That left two days to cover ninety miles, measured as the goose flies. There was but one beast in the big timber that could travel like this. Antoine glanced furtively at Pierre, and the latter gave the faintest nod. "Loup Garou," their lips signalled.

Sebastien got up, stretched himself, gave a short laugh and strode to the door. "For a good dinner, *bien merci, mon vieux*. It is I who shall feed you when the logs come down past Villeneuve in the spring. Every woman of the family of Fisette is an incomparable cook. We shall be ready, Marie and I."

For a moment after he disappeared there was silence in the camp, till both men stepped quickly to the window. Sebastien had reached the ice, and putting on his snowshoes already struck southward across Lac St. Luc. He walked swiftly, dwindling as they watched to a dark speck that vanished round a nearby point. Then Antoine looked at his friend and swore a great oath.

"Jean — where is Jean?"

"He comes with the sawyers in ten minutes. But wait, I will call them now."

Pierre went out and smote with a poker on a large steel triangle that hung close to the door. Straightway the woods throbbed with a clear singing note that lifted through the green tops and caused a dropping of axes and cessation of droning saws, till down the winter roads trooped the lumberjacks, hungry as bears and chanting musically of Alluette and La Claire Fontaine. At their head came Jean Deslormes, a young, tawny-haired giant, straight as a hemlock and shouldered like a bull moose. He caught sight of Antoine outside the camp, and, running forward, flung round him a pair of gigantic arms.

"Ah, *c'est le vieux* Papa Carnot. When didst thou arrive, and hast thou perchance been at a place called Villeneuve?"

Antoine struggled for breath. "I would first that some young fools learn their strength — and use it less," he gasped — then, in a whisper, "No, I have not visited Villeneuve since a fortnight past, but —"

"A fortnight! That is but a moment, while I have not been there for two months. Is there nothing then to tell me, no message?"

"Shout not thy love to the whole camp, my son. There was one here a moment ago who even now is on his way to Villeneuve."

"Have you then sold all your stock to the good Pierre, and send out for more?"

Antoine shook his head. "The name of the traveller is Sebastien, and he goes fast."

"Le Loup Garou," said Jean grimly. "But why to Villeneuve?"

"In search of one Marie Fisette, who he swears will be his in the space of five days. My son will need all his strength, and must act very quickly. Let go, Jean, you break my arm!"

"He took what trail? — quick!" Jean swayed a little, with such a tremor as runs through the brown column of a pine when the saw eats at its heart.

"He said that his trail was his own, and that any might follow who could, then struck south around the point. Shut up they Marie in they breast, my son, and hasten; but" — and here Antoine sent him an eloquent glance — "search not always for the form of a man as you travel."

Jean hurled himself into the sleeping-camp.

In ten minutes he was out on the ice, and, clearing the strewn logs, swung forward toward the first southerly point of Lac St. Luc. Thus led Sebastien's trail — long, narrow tracks with the points of the shoes turned up a little more than was usual in a bush country and the tail of one with an outward twist. He would remember that. They took him round that point, straight as an arrow-flight past the next one and on to a glassy patch where the water had come up and turned a mile of Lac St. Luc into a looking-glass. Here he slipped off his shoes, trotted across, and cast about close to the shore line. There was no more trail.

He stood for a moment, shaking his head like a great, puzzled dog. This was the trail that any might follow who could! His lips became dry as he doubled back, and, picking up his own tracks, traversed the edge of the patch till he came to them again. "By Gar!" he whispered. "By Gar!"

Eighty miles due south was Villeneuve, with Marie and tinkling sleigh bells and pearl-grey smoke climbing from heaped roofs. Somewhere to the south was something nosing swiftly through the big timber. "Search not always for the form of a man," Antoine had said. Jean jerked out a tense petition to St. Joseph, patron and guardian of the family Fisette, then put on his shoes.

There was moonlight by seven. It turned the snow to a pale purple, on which blue-black shadows of big timber lay in wide and parallel bars. He tramped across these, bar to bar, leaning forward with massive arms swinging, his legs working like pistons; a vast engine of a man moving in a white flurry and spouting deep-drawn jets of vapour. There was no sound save the creak of shoes, and a muffled thud as some overburdened cedar doffed its load of snow and straightened its tender branches in the stinging air. Presently he came to a frozen swamp. On the other side of this, where the shadows began again, stood a lone wolf.

It vanished as he started, merging like one shadow into another. Jean paused for a moment while a new thought dawned, and struck off sharp to the right. Two hundred yards away he found it — a wolf track — the triangular pad with the long sharp projecting toe and narrow trailing heel. He followed this back a quarter-mile, noting that it paralleled his own, curving where his curved and holding south for Villeneuve. And then Jean knew.

At four in the morning the moon went down in a bank of cloud. Came a whine of wind and a few drifting flakes. The woods grew dark. By this time Jean was very hungry, and therefore felt cold, for in these latitudes the body, like a boiler, demands fuel. He shovelled aside the snow, made fire and tea, searching the gloom with quick and furtive glances, crossing himself between gulps. In ten minutes he heard a rabbit squeal. That meant death in the ground hemlock near by. Something else was feeding there, and resting — resting.

As the goose flies it is ninety miles from the camp on St. Luc to Villeneuve, but a man travels not less than a hundred. As a wolf might go it is perhaps ninety-five. At sunrise Jean knew it was the same this time for man and wolf. There was not so much concealment now. He saw the gaunt, grey form flitting, wraith-like, between brown trunks, a malign beast with deep, lean shoulders and bony, arrow-shaped head. It rested when he rested, ate when he ate — and kept always a little in advance. By mid-afternoon it became difficult to think of anything else and he grew very sleepy. It was only the vision of Marie with her flaxen hair, her smiling mouth and white arms that held him awake. At sundown he knew that he must sleep if only for half an hour, or he would lose his way. There were no stars this time, and no moon. He made two fires of green birch logs, laid spruce boughs between them, pulled the hood of his capote over his nose and stretched out.

Instantly, it seemed he began to dream. There was no loup garou now, but only love and the whiteness of his girl's shoulder. At this junction his body yielded, his great muscles relaxed; till, smiling, he plunged into an abyss of slumber, lulled by tiny, crepitant voices from the surrounding forest. Then, horribly, the dream became distorted. Marie's face, so close to his own, changed to a grinning mask with black lifted lips, flat, sleek skull, and malevolent yellow eyes. The yellow gave place to black. They were the eyes of Sebastien. Simultaneously came a strange warmth on his cheeks. He blinked. Something was staring at him, something so near that it shut out the rest of the world. He gave a cry and sprang to his feet. There was a scramble in the snow by the spruce boughs. Jean Deslormes was alone again.

"*Que le bon Dieu nous sauvais!*" he whispered, trembling.

From a southward ridge came answer, not by *le bon Dieu*, but the wild and haunting voice of the grey wolf. Through the big timber it drifted, savage, remote, but inescapable, the note of terror that in a season of the year carries its own message to fur and hide on the foothills of the Laurentians. To Jean it also carried a message, and he flung himself to Villeneuve. He swung on, summoning his vast reserve of strength, plunging through underbrush where once he would have gone round, himself now a thing of the woods in the manner of his going — this giant with the mind of a child. He stayed not to rest or eat; he looked not again for the grey shape. Then a remembered hilltop — a winter road for drawing wood — an outlying pasture — the bark of a distant dog — and below, in the valley, revealed in the half-light of dawn, the spire of a church and the forty farms they called Villeneuve. Into the crisping air climbed forty pencils of pearl smoke, like the exhalations of those who slumbered yet a while ere facing the rigour of the day.

Jean tore downhill to the house of Marthe Fisette, the mother of Marie. It seemed that all was safe here. He paused at the door, heard inside the crackling of a fire, and knocked. At sight of him the old woman dropped an armful of wood.

"Jean!" she stammered, "how came you here?"

"As flies the goose from Lac St. Luc," he said, breathing hard; "and Marie?"

Marthe did not answer that, but stared at him wonderingly and with a touch of awe. "It is undoubtedly the good God who has sent you, but how did you know?"

"Antoine Carnot told me; and, hearing it, I waited for nothing —" He broke off, staring back. "Then it is true?"

"Sebastien?" Her lips framed the name.

He nodded. "Le Loup Garou! Together we have come from the camp on Lac St. Luc, and this morning he also is in Villeneuve, but in what form I know not. Last night when for a moment I closed my eyes he came and crouched beside me, breathing in my face, and would have torn my throat had I not suddenly awakened. I brought no gun, for one cannot kill a loup garou except with a bullet that has been blessed, and there was no priest on Lac St. Luc."

Marthe crossed herself fervently. "That is true — always it has been so."

"And the friends here — what do they say?"

"They shrug their shoulders — and say nothing. It is not well to quarrel with Sebastien. There is that affair of the good Famieux — a thing all remember."

"And Marie?" he demanded.

Marthe sent him a wintry smile. "Look over your shoulder, my son."

She was halfway down the ladder stair from the room above; Marie with thick, yellow, knitted strands down her back, great, slumberous roses in her smooth cheeks, and drowsy love in her blue eyes. Jean gave a huge, gusty sigh of delight, put out his mighty arms and lifted her as one picks up an acorn. She hid her face in his capote.

"My little one," he said softly, "my little partridge; thou art safe here, very safe."

Presently they put food before him, and he ate ravenously, telling in snatches of the trip from Lac St. Luc — "ninety-five miles in forty-two hours, by Gar!" — while Marie clucked over him as though she were indeed a hen partridge, and Marthe busied herself without words between stove and table. Then Jean got up.

"I go now to Père Leduc, for we shall be married in three days. Also there is the matter of blessing some bullets." He paused, and waved a hand at the encircling bush. "It is there I shall use them."

"I also shall go," said Marie, divided between love and fear.

He shook his great head. "Such talk is not for my little bird, but thou shalt go so far as the store, and wait there. In three days my soul shall go everywhere with me. Be content, my swallow."

They went off down the packed road, where the snowplough had left four-foot ridges on either side, down to the store which was diagonally opposite the church and the house of the good Father. Here Jean left her clasped to the expansive bosom of Madame Famieux, crossed the road, kicked his shoepacks clean and found Père Leduc in his book-lined study. And books were precious north of the Laurentians. He spoke first of his heart's desire.

The Father nodded, smiling. He loved this young Anak, this son of the wilderness, with his great thews and childlike heart. Wise and tender was Père Leduc, a pure flame that glowed constantly, healing both minds and souls with a wide spiritual paternity.

"It is well for you both — and the good Marthe agrees?"

Jean nodded.

"Then I will call your names at vespers this very night, so that it may take place in three days. A good girl, your Marie. You go yourself back to Lac St. Luc?"

No, Jean would not do that. He had saved eight hundred dollars for a farm — and the farm of Georges Laurier was it not in the market? He paused a moment.

"There is another matter, *mon père* — that of these bullets." He held out a dozen, cupped in a gigantic palm. "May it please you to bless them?"

Père Leduc shook his head gently. Were he not very wise he would have laughed. He knew — knew all about it. Individually he knew more than the entire village put together. Part of his strength was that he only revealed a fraction of his knowledge. And now he wanted to hear what this enormous child had to say — all of it.

"Tell me, my son."

Jean told him, from the very start, touching not on the physical marvel of the trip — for to Jean it was no marvel — but only on its terror. How did Sebastien leave the flooded patch on Lac St. Luc? What became of his shoes when he turned into a wolf? What did he mean by breathing in Jean's face? Why did he lead the way to

Villeneuve? And most of all, what was the import of his boast about Marie? There must be an end to this — the end brought by a bullet that had been blessed. All Villeneuve was waiting for that.

Père Leduc put his hand on the young giant's shoulder, and spoke of tradition and legends and the powers of evil. "No, my son, you yourself are about to give answer to Sebastien — a final answer. You and this dear daughter of the parish will have my blessing, and not these bullets. When in three days you leave the church with Marie on your arm and joy in your heart you will have replied to Sebastien. He will have written himself down as a loud-speaking fool at whom not only the village of Villeneuve will laugh. That laugh will run up and down the Saguenay, till he will wish to walk into the stream itself to escape it. As for what you saw and searched for, but did not find on your way here, when the mind of a man be distraught with weariness, and perhaps fear, there is not much of which he can be very sure. You have had an evil dream, but it is past. Go now, my son, and take peace and happiness with you. *Le bon Dieu* is not forgetful of His children on the Saguenay."

Jean went out, cheered but not convinced. It was all very well to talk like that. But he *knew*, while the good Father had not been on the trail from St. Luc. He rubbed the bullets together in his pocket, stalked across to the store and gathered in Marie.

"Behold my wife in three days — this little spruce partridge," he said to the fat Madame Famieux. "*Vien donc, chérie;* there is much to talk of."

Up the shining road, arms linked, they walked, while Jean told her the words of Père Leduc. Nor was Marie convinced. The good Father had never felt Sebastien's burning eyes, nor could he understand what it meant to a girl to shrink and quiver beneath that insolent stare till she became weak and helpless like a bird in a net.

"It is but one thing we shall do, Jean."

"What is that, my dove?"

"You shall meet Sebastien and take his promise, or make it, that there is an end to all this."

"Of what value then is the word of a wolf? Could he speak it?" grunted Jean. Then, looking up, his heart leaped. Sebastien had rounded a bend in the road and came straight toward them. Marie saw him, shivered, and clung closer.

"Jean," she whispered, "not now!"

Drawing nearer he walked more slowly, staring first at the giant with strange, inscrutable gaze, then at Marie with a wild, unhuman hunger. His cheeks were hollow, but he moved lightly on his feet. They were not the feet of a man who has travelled ninety miles in forty-two hours — or less. He came level with them. Marie found herself pushed gently forward and past him. Jean stood motionless, every sinew in him turned to fire.

"Loup Garou," he said thickly. "Loup Garou, what seek you now?"

Sebastien did not speak, but lowered his lids, and from hot, half-veiled eyes sent the big man a look of contemptuous pity. So keen was it, so utterly penetrating, that Jean felt as though a hand were fumbling in his breast and groping for secrets. Then, as Sebastien was about to pass on, a mighty arm shot out and took him by the throat. He was shaken as a wolverine shakes a rabbit, shaken till his teeth chattered and flung headlong into the crusted snow. Jean turned on his heel and followed Marie.

"It is done, my turtle — and the wolf did not bark."

Late that night, after Jean had gone to sleep at the farm of Christophe Famieux, Marie talked long with her mother and told her the words of Père Leduc. Marthe could make no answer to these words, but found them nevertheless devoid of comfort. Presently she climbed the stair ladder, returning with a small image of St. Joseph, patron saint to every good Fisette.

"It is lead," she murmured, "and from Ste. Anne de Beaupré it came, where it was blessed by his Eminence from Quebec. Is it not that the head of the holy man is of the size of a bullet?

Marie nodded, her eyes brightening.

"Then the rest of it I leave to thee, my pigeon. When thy mountain of a husband shall take thee from me in a sleigh to Beaulieu on the third day from this, see that the short gun of Christophe be thus loaded, and near at hand under the robes. It is in my mind that there will be need of that gun."

So on the third day, Gaston Roubidoux, sacristan, sent a rocking peal from the wooden church, and those of Villeneuve came in box-like sleighs stuffed with straw, and drawn by short-legged, round-bodied Percheron horses, to see the union of Jean and Marie — doubly intriguing because it spelled the humiliation of Le Loup Garou. Marie was all in white, with everlastings in her hair; Jean in a new, tight and very bright blue suit into which he just wedged his great body, celluloid collar anchored by a large rolled-gold stud, yellow tie, and patent leather shoes that hurt abominably. Then Père Leduc spoke words of peace and love, after which they all went to the house of Christophe, the largest in the village, where was given the marriage feast, with riotous quadrilles and great good feeling. And Sebastien had not been seen by anyone since three days — which added not a little to the general hilarity.

Beaulieu lay thirty miles away — or was it only three? Jean, being dizzy with happiness and pride, was not quite sure when at sunset he tucked his girl into the sleigh, wrapping the robes closely round her feet. There was plenty of straw underneath. Marthe had seen to that. The horses, pet team of Christophe, arching their glossy necks, dashed off with a jangle of bells and laughter and cheers. The good Father nodded contentedly and turned homeward. These children of his — how gay and handsome they were!

Halfway to Beaulieu — the horses going like playful kittens — Marie pressing to his side — frosty roses in her cheeks — the blue eyes like stars — with all this Jean could hardly believe his own good fortune. What a noble day it had been, and how many others, even more wonderful, lay ahead! His feet were now very sore — that being from the dancing — his collar stud was boring a hole in his gullet, but he was bursting with joy.

"My love," he breathed, "my soul — my little ptarmigan!"

Just at this moment there came from a belt of cedar hard by, the pulsing howl of a timber wolf. Marie heard and shivered. Jean heard, and his heart stopped, then began to race. The Percherons heard, whinnied their alarm, and plunged forward. Jean, gripping the reins, lashed out till the woods streamed past in a blur. If the road only held open he could make Beaulieu in an hour.

They swung into a clearing where the wind had got at the snow and the road was drifted level. Knee-deep toiled the Percherons, heads down, backs rippled with straining muscles. Jean stood up. Something shot across just ahead, turned, doubled back, and made a ripping, darting stroke at the throat of the nearest horse.

"Quick, Jean, under the straw at my feet — the gun of Christophe with the head of St. Joseph!" panted Marie.

He wondered what St. Joseph had to do with it, but a gun was a gun, and, burrowing swiftly, he recognized the short, single-barrelled muzzle-loader with half-inch bore. Pushing the reins into the girl's hands, he cuddled his cheek against the brown stock — and waited. The near Percheron was bleeding at the throat. Again that lean, darting form, ears flattened back on the sleek skull, again the curving attack rapid as light.

The wolf was in mid-air when the foresight covered a grey shoulder for a fraction of time. Jean crooked his finger — saw horses rearing in a tangle of harness — heard Marie cry out in a jangle of bells. Then a long, hairy body seemed to have been thrust away, and stretched, twitching, just ahead of the driving hoofs.

He snatched back the reins, forced on the Percherons and fetched them up, quivering, on top of the thing on the road. Here for a deadly second the steel-shod, dancing feet hammered down — down, till what lay beneath was a shapeless lump of bloody hide. Marie covered her eyes, but Jean, soothing his team, stared at it hard before he bent over and kissed the roses back to her cheeks. It was in his mind that the eyes of this wolf, instead of being long and yellow, had been large and dark and burning. They did not burn now. But he said nothing of this.

"My little weasel spoke of the gun of Christophe with the head of the good St. Joseph," he smiled. "And what did she mean by that?"

Marie told him, and for months after that there was little talk of Sebastien. Then summer arrived. The logs from St. Luc began to come down the Saguenay, and Jean was persuaded to help the drive through the chute of Les Arables. Marie went with him, and so it happened that Pierre Colange on a certain day did indeed sit at the table of an incomparable cook. The shanty that Jean knocked together stood close to the river, and the table was outside. They were talking of Sebastien when Pierre got up, shaded his eyes and stared hard at the tawny water.

"It has been in my mind, *mon vieux*, that we should meet him yet once again. What is that between the two hemlocks?"

He had come down with the logs, — come from the unknown — and circled slowly in a great eddy. The smooth face was still unscarred. One sodden arm rested slack on the ribbed bark. The eddy brought him toward shore, bobbing as though something were twitching at his heels. The three gazed at each other, till Jean, remembering the prophecy of Père Leduc, lifted his brows and signalled.

"Go inside a moment, my little beaver. It is not for thee to see."

There is a cross underneath a jack-pine just below that eddy. Jean hewed it. On a flat stone at the foot is a small leaden image without a head. That was the thought of Marie. On the cross Pierre

Colange, with some misgivings, put the name — one word. He could not decide what else, under the circumstances, one might safely say. It stood there after the drive went on and the following sweep had cleared every stranded log. Squirrels perched on it, rabbits hopped about it, red-headed woodpeckers sometimes tried their strength on its tough fibre. But nothing happened till Antoine Carnot passed in the autumn.

He saw it, read the one word and exactly appreciated the difficulty. So, smiling, he lit his pipe, squatted close, and began to carve with firm, deep strokes.

"Sebastien. Le Loup Garou," read the next lumberjack who came that way.

This page intentionally left blank

THE FLOOD

by
Sir Gilbert Parker
from *Pierre and His People: Tales of the Far North*. Toronto: Copp
Clark, 1897.

"Truth will come to light; murder cannot be hid long."
The Merchant of Venice

"The Flood," a highly melodramatic tale, has been praised for its haunting
quality. Pretty Pierre, the half-breed, is the villain-cum-hero of these tales.

This page intentionally left blank

Wendling came to Fort Anne on that day that the Reverend Ezra Badgley and an unknown girl were buried. And that was a notable thing. The man had been found dead at his evening meal; the girl had died on the same day. And they were buried side by side. This caused much scandal, for the man was holy, and the girl, as many women said, was probably evil altogether. At the graves, when the minister's people saw what was being done, they piously protested; but the Factor, to whom Pierre had whispered a word, answered them gravely that the matter should go on, since none knew but the woman was as worthy of heaven as the man. Wendling chanced to stand beside Pretty Pierre.

"Who knows!" he said aloud, looking hard at the graves. "Who knows!... She died before him, but the dead can strike."

Pierre did not answer immediately, for the Factor was calling the earth down on both coffins; but after a moment he added: "Yes, the dead can strike." And then the eyes of the two men caught and stayed, and they knew that they had things to say to each other in the world.

They became friends. And that, perhaps, was not greatly to Wendling's credit; for in the eyes of many Pierre was an outcast as an outlaw. Maybe some of the women disliked this friendship most; since Wendling was a handsome man, and Pierre was never known to seek them, good or bad; and they blamed him for the other's coldness, for his unconcerned yet respectful eye.

"There's Nelly Nolan would dance after him to the world's end," said Shon McGann to Pierre one day; "and the Widdy Jerome herself, wid her flamin' cheeks and the wild fun in her eye, croons like a babe at the breast as he slides out his cash on the bar; and over on Gansonby's Flat there's —"

"There's many a fool," sharply interjected Pierre, as he pushed the needle through a button he was sewing on his coat.

"Bedad, there's a pair of fools here, anyway, said I; for the women might die without lift at waist or brush of lip, and neither of ye'd say, 'Here's to the joy of us, goddess, me own!'"

Pierre seemed to be intently watching the needle point as it pierced up the button-eye, and his reply was given with a slowness corresponding to the sedate passage of the needle. "Wendling, you think, cares nothing for women? Well, men who are like that cared once for one woman, and when that was over — but, pshaw! I will not talk. You are no thinker, Shon McGann. You blunder through the world. And you'll tremble as much to a woman's thumb in fifty years as now."

"By the holy smoke," said Shon, "though I tremble at that, maybe, I'll not tremble, as Wendling, at nothing at all." Here Pierre looked up sharply, then dropped his eyes on his work again. Shon lapsed suddenly into a moodiness.

"Yes," said Pierre, "as Wendling, at nothing at all? Well?"

"Well, this, Pierre, for you that's a thinker from me that's none. I was walking with him in Red Glen yesterday. Sudden he took to shiverin', and snatched me by the arm, and a mad look shot out of his handsome face. 'Hush!' says he. I listened. There was a sound like the hard rattle of a creek over stones, and then another sound behind that. 'Come quick,' says he, the sweat standin' thick on him; and he ran me up the bank — for it was at the beginnin' of the Glen where the sides were low — and there we stood pantin' and starin' flat at each other. 'What's that? and what's got its hand on ye? for y' are as cold as death, an' pinched in the face, an' you've bruised my arm,' said I. And he looked round him slow and breathed hard, then drew his fingers through the sweat on his cheek. 'I'm not well, and I thought I heard — you heard it; what was it like?' said he; and he peered close at me. 'Like water,' said I, 'a little creek near, and a flood comin' far off.' 'Yes, just like that,' said he; 'it's some trick of wind in the place, but it makes a man foolish, and an inch of brandy would be the right thing.' I didn't say No to that. An on we came, and brandy we had with a wish in the eye of Nelly Nolan that'd warm the heart of a tomb.... And there's a cud for your chewin', Pierre. Think that by the neck and the tail, and the divil absolve you."

During this, Pierre had finished with the button. He had drawn on his coat and lifted his hat, and now lounged, trying the point of the needle with his forefinger. When Shon ended, he said with a sidelong glance: "But what did *you* think of all that, Shon?"

"Think! There it was! What's the use of thinkin'? There's many a trick in the world with wind or with spirit, as I've seen often enough in ould Ireland, and it's not to be guessed by me." Here his voice got a little lower and a trifle solemn. "For Pierre," spoke he, "there's what's more than life or death, and sorra wan can we tell what it is; but we'll know some day whin —"

"When we've taken the leap at the Almighty Ditch," said Pierre, with a grave kind of lightness. "Yes, it is all strange. But even the Almighty Ditch is worth the doing; nearly everything is worth the doing; being young, growing old, fighting, loving — when youth is on — hating, eating, drinking, working, playing big games: all is worth it except two things."

"And what are they, bedad?"

"Thy neighbour's wife. Murder. — Those are horrible. They double on a man one time or another; always."

Here, as in curiosity, Pierre pierced his finger with the needle, and watched the blood form in a little globule. Looking at it meditatively and sardonically, he said: "There is only one end to these. Blood for blood is a great matter; and I used to wonder if it would not be terrible for a man to see his death advancing on him drop by drop, like that." And he let the spot of blood fall to the floor. "But now I know that there is a punishment worse than that ... *mon Dieu!* worse than that," he added.

Into Shon's face a strange look had suddenly come. "Yes, there's something worse than that, Pierre."

"So, *bien?*"

Shon made the sacred gesture of his creed. "To be punished by
the dead. And not see them — only hear them." And his eyes
steadied firmly to the other's.

Pierre was about to reply, but there came the sound of footsteps
through the open door, and presently Wendling entered slowly. He
was pale and worn, and his eyes looked out with a searching
anxiousness. But that did not render him less comely. He had always
dressed in black and white, and this now added to the easy and yet
severe refinement of his person. His birth and breeding had occurred
in places unfrequented by such as Shon and Pierre; but plains and
wild life level all; and men are friends according to their taste and
will, and by no other law. Hence these with Wendling. He stretched
out his hand to each without a word. The handshake was unusual;
he had little demonstration ever. Shon looked up surprised, but
responded. Pierre followed with a swift, inquiring look; then, in the
succeeding pause, he offered cigarettes. Wendling took one; and all,
silent, sat down. The sun streamed intemperately through the
doorway, making a broad ribbon of light straight across the floor to
Wendling's feet. After lighting his cigarette, he looked into the
sunlight for a moment, still not speaking. Shon meanwhile had
started his pipe, and now, as if he found the silence awkward — "It's
a day for God's country, this," he said: "to make man a Christian for
little or much, though he play with the Divil betune whiles."
Without looking at them, Wendling said, in a low voice: "It was just
such a day, down there in Quebec, when it happened. You could
hear the swill of the river, and the water licking the piers, and the
saws in the Big Mill and the Little Mill as they marched through the
timer, flashing their teeth like bayonets. It's a wonderful sound on a
hot, clear day — that wild, keen singing of the saws, like the cry of a
live thing fighting and conquering. Up from the fresh-cut lumber in
the yards there came a smell like the juice of apples, and the
sawdust, as you thrust your hand into it, was as cool and soft as the
leaves of a clove flower in the dew. On these days the town was
always still. It looked sleeping, and you saw the heat quivering up
from the wooden walls and the roofs of cedar shingles as though the
houses were breathing."

Here he paused, still intent on the shaking sunshine. Then he
turned to the others as if suddenly aware that he had been talking
to them. Shon was about to speak, but Pierre threw a restraining

glance, and, instead, they all looked through the doorway and beyond. In the settlement below they saw the effect that Wendling had described. The houses breathed. A grasshopper went clacking past, a dog at the door snapped up a fly; but there seemed no other life of day. Wendling nodded his head towards the distance. "It was quiet, like that. I stood and watched the mills and the yards, and listened to the saws, and looked at the great slide, and the logs on the river: and I said ever to myself that it was all mine; all. Then I turned to a big house on the hillock beyond the cedars, whose windows were open, with a cool dusk lying behind them. More than all else, I loved to think I owned that house and what was in it.... She was a beautiful woman. And she used to sit in a room facing the mill — though the house fronted another way — thinking of me, I did not doubt, and working at some delicate needle-stuff. There never had been a sharp word between us, save when I quarrelled bitterly with her brother, and he left the mill and went away. But she got over that mostly, though the lad's name was never mentioned between us. That day I was so hungry for the sight of her that I got my field glass — used to watch my vessels and rafts making across the bay — and trained it on the window where I knew she sat. I thought it would amuse her, too, when I went back at night, if I told her what she had been doing. I laughed to myself at the thought of it as I adjusted the glass.... I looked.... There was no more laughing.... I saw her, and in front of her a man, with his back half on me. I could not recognize him, though at the instant I thought he was something familiar. I failed to get his face at all. Hers I found indistinctly. But I saw him catch her playfully by the chin! After a little they rose. He put his arm about her and kissed her, and he ran his fingers through her hair. She had such fine golden hair; so light, and lifted to every breath.... Something got into my brain. I know now it was the maggot which sent Othello mad. The world in that hour was malicious, awful....

"After a time — it seemed ages: she and everything had receded so far — I went ... home. At the door I asked the servant who had been there. She hesitated, confused, and then said the young curate of the parish. I was very cool: for madness is a strange thing; you see everything with an intense aching clearness — that is the trouble.... She was more kind than common. I do not think I was unusual. I was playing a part well — my grandmother had Indian blood like yours, Pierre — and I was waiting. I was even nicely critical of her to myself. I balanced the mole on her neck against her general beauty; the curve of her instep, I decided, was a little too emphatic. I passed her back and forth before me, weighing her at every point; but yet these two things were the only imperfections. I pronounced her an exceeding piece of art — and infamy. I was much interested to see how she could appear perfect in her soul. I encouraged her to talk. I saw with devilish irony that an angel spoke. And, to cap it all, she assumed the fascinating air of the mediator — for her brother; seeking a reconciliation between us. Her amazing art of person and mind so worked upon me that it became unendurable; it was so exquisite — and so shameless. I was sitting where the priest had sat that afternoon; and when she leaned towards me I caught her chin lightly and trailed my fingers through her hair as he had done: and that ended it, for I was cold, and my heart worked with horrible slowness. Just as a wave poises at its height before breaking upon the shore, it hung at every pulsebeat, and then seemed to fall over with a sickening thud. I arose, and, acting still, spoke impatiently of her brother. Tears sprang to her eyes. Such divine dissimulation, I thought — too good for earth. She turned to leave the room, and I did not stay her. Yet we were together again that night.... I was only waiting."

The cigarette had dropped from his fingers to the floor, and lay there smoking. Shon's face was fixed with anxiety; Pierre's eyes played gravely with the sunshine. Wendling drew a heavy breath, and then went on.

"Again, next day, it was like this — the world draining the heat.... I watched from the Big Mill. I saw them again. He leaned over her chair and buried his face in her hair. The proof was absolute now.... I started away, going a roundabout, that I might not be seen. It took me some time. I was passing through a clump of cedar when I saw them making towards the trees skirting the river. Their backs were on me. Suddenly they diverted their steps towards the great slide, shut off from water this last few months, and used as a quarry to deepen it. Some petrified things had been found in the rocks, but I did not think they were going to these. I saw them climb down the rocky steps; and presently they were lost to view. The gates of the slide could be opened by machinery from the Little Mill. A terrible, deliciously malignant thought came to me. I remember how the sunlight crept away from me and left me in the dark. I stole through that darkness to the Little Mill. I went to the machinery for opening the gates. Very gently I set it in motion, facing the slide as I did so. I could see it through the open sides of the mill. I smiled to think what the tiny creek, always creeping through a faint leak in the gates and falling with a granite rattle on the stones, would now become. I pushed the lever harder — harder. I saw the gates suddenly give, then fly open, and the river sprang roaring massively through them. I heard a shriek through the roar. I shuddered; and a horrible sickness came on me.... And as I turned from the machinery, I saw the young priest coming at me through a doorway!... It was not the priest and my wife that I had killed; but my wife and her brother...."

He threw his head back as though something clamped his throat. His voice roughened with misery: "The young priest buried them both, and people did not know the truth. They were even sorry for me. But I gave up the mills — all; and I became homeless ... this."

Now he looked up at the two men, and said: "I have told you because you know something, and because there will, I think, be an end soon." He got up and reached out a trembling hand for a cigarette. Pierre gave him one. "Will you walk with me?" he asked.

Shon shook his head. "God forgive you!" he replied. "I can't do it."

But Wendling and Pierre left the hut together. They walked for an hour, scarcely speaking, and not considering where they went. At last Pierre mechanically turned to go down into Red Glen. Wendling stopped short, then, with a sighing laugh, strode on. "Shon has told you what happened here?" he said.

Pierre nodded.

"And you know what came once when you walked with me.... The dead can strike," he added.

Pierre sought his eye. "The minister and the girl buried together that day," he said, "were —"

He stopped, for behind him he heard the sharp, cold trickle of water. Silent they walked on. It followed them. They could not get out of the Glen now until they had compassed its length — the walls were high. The sound grew. The men faced each other. "Goodbye," said Wendling; and he reached out his hand swiftly. But Pierre heard a mighty flood groaning on them, and he blinded as he stretched his arm in response. He caught at Wendling's shoulder, but felt him lifted and carried away, while he himself stood still in a screeching wind and heard impalpable water rushing over him. In a minute it was gone; and he stood alone in Red Glen.

He gathered himself up and ran. The hands were wrinkled; the face was cold; the body was wet: the man was drowned and dead.

THE GOLD WOLF

by
William Alexander Fraser
from *Bulldog Carney*. New York: George H. Doran, 1919.

The linked stories in *Bulldog Carney* are skilfully told Western tales about a Robin Hood-like smuggler in the Alberta foothills and the British Columbia interior. This story is set in the Kootenay District of B.C.

This page intentionally left blank

A ll day long Bulldog Carney had found, where the trail was soft, the odd imprint of that goblined, inturned hoof. All day in the saddle — riding a trail that winds in and out among rocks, and trees, and cliffs monotonously similar, the hush of the everlasting hills holding in subjection man's soul, the towering giants of embattled rocks thrusting up towards God's dome pigmying to nothingness that rat, a man — produces a comatose condition of mind; man becomes a child, incapable of little beyond the recognition of trivial things; the erratic swoop of a bird, the sudden roar of a cataract, the dirge-like sigh of wind through the harp of a giant pine.

And so, curiously, Bulldog's fancy had toyed aimlessly with the history of the cayuse that owned that inturned left forefoot. Always where the hoof's imprint lay was the flat track of a miner's boot, the hobnails denting the black earth with stolid persistency. But the owner of the miner's boot seemed of little moment; it was the abnormal hoof that, by a strange perversity, haunted Carney.

The man was probably a placer miner coming down out of the Eagle Hills, leading a pack pony that carried his duffel and, perhaps, a small fortune in gold. Of course, like Carney, he was heading for steel, for the town of Bucking Horse.

Toward evening, as Carney rode down a winding trail that led to the ford of Singing Water, rounding an abrupt turn the mouth of a huge cave yawned in the side of a cliff away to his left. Something of life had melted into its dark shadow that had the semblance of a man; or it might have been a bear or a wolf. Lower down in the valley that was called the Valley of the Grizzley's Bridge, his buckskin shied, and with a snort of fear left the trail and elliptically came back to it twenty yards beyond.

In the centre of the ellipse, on the trail, stood a gaunt form, a huge dog-wolf. He was a sinister figure, his snarling lips curled back from strong yellow fangs, his wide powerful head low hung, and the black bristles on his back erect in challenge.

The whole thing was weird, uncanny; a single wolf to stand his ground in daylight was unusual.

Instinctively Bulldog reined in the buckskin, and half turning in the saddle, with something of a shudder, searched the ground at the wolf's feet dreading to find something. But there was nothing.

The dog-wolf, with a snarling twist of his head, sprang into the bushes just as Carney dropped a hand to his gun; his quick eye had seen the movement.

Carney had meant to camp just beyond the ford of Singing Water, but the usually placid buckskin was fretful, nervous.

A haunting something was in the air; Carney, himself, felt it. The sudden apparition of the wolf could not account for this mental unrest, either in man or beast, for they were both inured to the trail, and a wolf meant little beyond a skulking beast that a pistol shot would drive away.

High above the rider towered Old Squaw Mountain. It was like a battered feudal castle, on its upper reaches turret and tower and bastion catching vagrant shafts of gold and green, as, beyond, in the far west, a flaming sun slid down behind the Selkirks. Where he rode in the twisted valley a chill had struck the air, suggesting vaults, dungeons; the giant ferns hung heavy like the plumes of knights drooping with the death dew. A reaching stretch of salmon bushes studded with myriad berries that gleamed like topaz jewels hedged on both sides the purling, frothing stream that still held the green tint of its glacier birth.

Many times in his opium running Carney had swung along this wild trail almost unconscious of the way, his mind travelling far afield; now back to the old days of club life; to the years of army routine; to the bright and happy scenes where rich-gowned women and cultured men laughed and bantered with him. At times it was the newer rough life of the West; the ever-present warfare of man against man; the yesterday where he had won, or the tomorrow where he might cast a losing hazard — where the dice might turn groggily from a six-spotted side to a deuce, and the thrower take a fall.

But tonight, as he rode, something of depression, of a narrow environment, of an evil one, was astride the withers of his horse; the mountains seemed to close in and oppress him. The buckskin, too, swung his heavy lop-ears irritably back and forth, back and forth. Sometimes one ear was pricked forward as though its owner searched the beyond, the now-glooming valley that, at a little distance, was but a blur, the other ear held backward as though it would drink in the sounds of pursuit.

Pursuit! That was the very thing. Instinctively the rider turned in his saddle, one hand on the horn, and held his piercing gray eyes on the back trail, searching for the embodiment of this fantasy. The unrest had developed that far into conception, something evil hovered on his trail, man or beast. But he saw nothing but the swaying kaleidoscope of tumbling forest shadows; rocks that, half gloomed, took fantastic forms; bushes that swayed with the rolling gait of a grizzly.

The buckskin had quickened his pace as if, tired though he was, he would go on beyond that valley of fear before they camped.

Where the trail skirted the brink of a cliff that had a drop of fifty feet, Carney felt the horse tremble, and saw him hug the inner wall; and, when they had rounded the point, the buckskin, with a snort of relief, clamped the snaffle in his teeth and broke into a canter.

"I wonder — by Jove!" and Bulldog, pulling the buckskin to a stand, slipped from his back, and searched the black-loamed trail.

"I believe you're right, Pat," he said, addressing the buckskin; "something happened back there."

He walked for a dozen paces ahead of the horse, his keen grey eyes on the earth. He stopped and rubbed his chin, thinking — thinking aloud.

"There are tracks, Patsy boy — moccasins; but we've lost our gunboat-footed friend. What do you make of that, Patsy — gone over the cliff? But that damn wolf's pugs are here; he's travelled up and down. By gad! Two of them!"

Then, in silence, Carney moved along the way, searching and pondering; cast into a curious, superstitious mood that he could not shake off. The inturned hoof-print had vanished, so the owner of the big feet that carried hobnailed boots did not ride.

Each time Carney stopped to bend down in the study of the trail the buckskin pushed at him fretfully with his soft muzzle and rattled the snaffle against his bridle teeth.

At last Carney stroked the animal's head reassuringly, saying: "You're quite right, pal — it's none of our business. Besides, we're a pair of old grannies imagining things."

But as he lifted to the saddle, Bulldog, like the horse, felt a compelling inclination to go beyond the Valley of the Grizzley's Bridge to camp for the night.

Even as they climbed to a higher level of flat land, from back on the trail that was now lost in the deepening gloom, came the howl of a wolf; and then, from somewhere beyond floated the answering call of the dog-wolf's mate — a whimpering, hungry note in her weird wail.

"Bleat, damn you!" Carney cursed softly; "if you bother us I'll sit by with a gun and watch Patsy boy kick you to death."

As if some genii of the hills had taken up and sent on silent waves his challenge, there came filtering through the pines and birch a snarling yelp.

"By gad!" and Carney cocked his ear, pulling the horse to a stand.

Then in the heavy silence of the wooded hills he pushed on again muttering, "There's something wrong about that wolf howl — it's different."

Where a big pine had showered the earth with cones till the covering was soft, and deep, and springy, and odorous like a perfumed mattress of velvet, he hesitated; but the buckskin, in the finer animal reasoning, pleaded with little inpatient steps and shakes of the head that they push on.

Carney yielded, saying softly: "Go on, kiddie boy; peace of mind is good dope for a sleep."

So it was ten o'clock when the two travellers, Carney and Pat, camped in an open, where the moon, like a silver mirror, bathed the earth in reassuring light. Here the buckskin had come to a halt, filled his lungs with the perfumed air in deep draughts, and turning his head half round had waited for his partner to dismount.

It was curious this man of steel nerve and flawless courage feeling at all the guidance of unknown threatenings, unexplainable disquietude. He did not even build a fire; but choosing a place where the grass was rich he spread his blanket beside the horse's picket pin.

Bulldog's life had provided him with different sleeping moods; it was a curious subconscious matter of mental adjustment before he slipped away from the land of knowing. Sometimes he could sleep like a tired labourer, heavily, unresponsive to the noise of turmoil; at other times, when deep sleep might cost him his life, his senses hovered so close to consciousness that a dried leaf scurrying before the wind would call him to alert action. So now he lay on his blanket, sometimes over the border of spirit land, and sometimes conscious of the buckskin's pull at the crisp grass. Once he came wide awake, with no movement but the lifting of his eyelids. He had heard nothing; and now the grey eyes, searching the moonlit plain, saw nothing. Yet within was a full consciousness that there was something — not close, but hovering there beyond.

The buckskin also knew. He had been lying down, but with a snort of discontent his forequarters went up and he canted to his feet with a spring of wariness. Perhaps it was the wolves.

But after a little Carney knew it was not the wolves; they, cunning devils, would have circled beyond his vision, and the buckskin, with his delicate scent, would have swung his head full circle of the compass; but he stood facing down the back trail; the thing was there, watching.

After that Carney slept again, lighter if possible, thankful that he had yielded to the wisdom of the horse and sought the open.

Half a dozen times there was this gentle transition from the sleep that was hardly a sleep, to a full acute wakening. And then the paling sky told that night was slipping off to the western ranges, and that beyond the Rockies, to the east, day was sleepily travelling in from the plains.

The horse was again feeding; and Carney, shaking off the lethargy of his broken sleep, gathered some dried stunted bushes, and, building a little fire, made a pot of tea; confiding to the buckskin as he mounted that he considered himself no end of a superstitious ass to have bothered over a nothing.

Not far from where Carney had camped the trail he followed turned to the left to sweep around a mountain, and here it joined, for a time, the trail running from Fort Steel west toward the Kootenay. The sun, topping the Rockies, had lifted from the earth the graying shadows, and now Carney saw, as he thought, the hoof-prints of the day before.

There was a feeling of relief with this discovery. There had been a morbid disquiet in his mind; a mental conviction that something had happened to that intoed cayuse and his huge-footed owner. Now all the weird fancies of the night had been just a vagary of mind. Where the trail was earthed, holding clear impressions, he dismounted, and walked ahead of the buckskin, reading the lettered clay. Here and there was imprinted a moccasined foot; once there was the impression of boots; but they were not the huge imprints of hobnailed soles. They showed that a man had dismounted, and then mounted again; and the cayuse had not an inturned left forefoot; also the toe wall of one hind foot was badly broken. His stride was longer, too; he did not walk with the short step of a pack pony.

The indefinable depression took possession of Bulldog again; he tried to shake it off — it was childish. The huge-footed one perhaps was a prospector, and had wandered up into some one of the gulches looking for gold. That was objecting Reason formulating a hypothesis.

Then presently Carney discovered the confusing element of the same cayuse tracks heading the other way, as if the man on horseback had travelled both up and down the trail.

Where the Bucking Horse trail left the Kootenay trail after circling the mountain, Carney saw that the hoof prints continued toward Kootenay. And there was a myriad of tracks; many mounted men had swung from the Bucking Horse trail to the Kootenay path; they had gone and returned, for the hoof prints that toed toward Bucking Horse lay on top.

This also was strange; men did not ride out from the sleepy old town in a troop like cavalry. There was but one explanation, the explanation of the West — those mounted men had ridden after somebody — had trailed somebody who was wanted quick.

This crescendo to his associated train of thought obliterated mentally the goblin-footed cayuse, the huge hobnailed boot, the something at the cliff, the hovering oppression of the night — everything.

Carney closed his mind to the torturing riddle and rode, sometimes humming an Irish ballad of Mangin's.

It was late afternoon when he rode into Bucking Horse; and Bucking Horse was in a ferment.

Seth Long's hotel, the Gold Nugget, was the cauldron in which the waters of unrest seethed.

A lynching was in a state of almost completion, with Jeanette Holt's brother, Harry, elected to play the leading part of the lynched. Through the deference paid to his well-known activity when hostile events were afoot, Carney was cordially drawn into the maelstrom of ugly-tempered men.

Jeanette's brother may be said to have suffered from a preponderance of opinion against him, for only Jeanette, and with less energy, Seth Long, were on his side. All Bucking Horse, angry Bucking Horse, was for stringing him up *tout de suite*. The times were propitious for this entertainment, for Sergeant Black, of the Mounted Police, was over at Fort Steel, or somewhere else on patrol, and the law was in the keeping of the mob.

Ostensibly Carney ranged himself on the side of law and order. This is what he meant when, leaning carelessly against the Nugget bar, one hand on his hip, chummily close to the butt of his six-gun, he said:

"This town had got a pretty good name, as towns go in the mountains, and my idea of a man that's too handy at the lynch game is that he's a pretty poor sport."

"How's that, Bulldog?" Kootenay Jim snapped.

"He's a poor sport," Carney drawled, "because he's got a hundred to one the best of it — first, last, and always; he isn't in any danger when he starts, because it's a hundred men to one poor devil, who, generally, isn't armed, and he knows that at the finish his mates will perjure themselves to save their own necks. I've seen one or two lynch mobs and they were generally egged on by men who were yellow."

Carney's gray eyes looked out over the room full of angry men with a quiet thoughtful steadiness that forced home the conviction that he was wording a logic he would demonstrate. No other man in that room could have stood up against that plank bar and declared himself without being called quick.

"You hear fust what this rat done, Bulldog, then we'll hear what you've got to say," Kootenay growled.

"That's well-spoken, Kootenay," Bulldog answered. "I'm fresh in off the trail, and perhaps I'm quieter than the rest of you, but first, being fresh in off the trail, there's a little custom to be observed."

With a sweep of his hand Carney waved a salute to a line of bottles behind the bar.

Jeanette, standing in the open door that led from the bar to the dining-room, gripping the door till her nails sank into the pine, felt hot tears gush into her eyes. How wise, how cool, this brave Bulldog that she loved so well. She had had no chance to plead with him for help. He had just come into that murder-crazed throng, and the words had been hurled at him from a dozen mouths that her brother Harry — Harry the waster, the no-good, the gambler — had been found to be the man who had murdered returning miners on the trail for their gold, and that they were going to string him up.

And now there he stood, her god of a man, Bulldog Carney, ranged on her side, calm, and brave. It was the first glint of hope since they had brought her brother in, bound to the back of a cayuse. She had pushed her way amongst the men, but they were wolves; she had pleaded and begged for delay, but the evidence was so overwhelming; absolutely hopeless it had appeared. But now something whispered "Hope."

It was curious the quieting effect that single drink at the bar had; the magnetism of Carney seemed to envelop the men, to make them reasonable. Ordinarily they were reasonable men. Bulldog knew this, and he played the card of reason.

For the two or three gunmen — Kootenay Jim, John of Slocan, and Denver Ike — Carney had his own terrible personality and his six-gun; he could deal with those three toughs if necessary.

"Now tell me, boys, what started this hellery?" Carney asked when they had drunk.

The story was fired at him; if a voice hesitated, another took up the narrative.

Miners returning from the gold field up in the Eagle Hills had mysteriously disappeared, never turning up at Bucking Horse. A man would have left the Eagle Hills, and somebody drifting in from the same place later on, would ask for him at Bucking Horse — nobody had seen him.

Then one after another two skeletons had been found on the trail; the bodies had been devoured by wolves.

"And wolves don't eat gold — not what you'd notice, as a steady chuck," Kootenay Jim yelped.

"Men wolves do," Carney thrust back, and his gray eyes said plainly, "That's your food, Jim."

"Meanin' what by that, pard?" Kootenay snarled, his face evil in a threat.

"Just what the words convey — you sort them out, Kootenay."

But Miner Graham interposed. "We got kinder leary about this wolf game, Carney, 'cause they ain't bothered nobody else 'cept men packin' in their winnin's from the Eagle Hills; and four days ago Caribou Dave — here he is sittin' right here — he arrives packin' Fourteen-foot Johnson — that is, all that's left of Fourteen-foot."

"Johnson was my pal," Caribou Dave interrupted, a quaver in his voice, "and he leaves the Eagle Nest two days ahead of me, packin' a big clean-up of gold on a cayuse. He was goin' to mooch around' Buckin' Horse till I creeps in afoot, then we was goin' out. We been together a good many years, ol' Fourteen-foot and me."

Something seemed to break in Caribou's voice and Graham added: "Dave finds his mate at the foot of a cliff."

Carney started; and instinctively Kootenay's hand dropped to his gun, thinking something was going to happen.

"I dunno just what makes me look there for Fourteen-foot, Bulldog," Caribou Dave explained, "I was comin' along the trail seein' the marks of 'em damn big feet of hisn, and they looked good to me — I guess I was getting' kinder homesick for him; when I'd camp I'd go out and paw 'em tracks; 'twas kinder like shakin' hands. We been together a good many years, buckin' the mountains and the plains, and sometimes havin' a bit of fun. I'm comin' along, as I says, and I sees a kinder scrimmage like, as if his old tan-coloured cayuse had got gay, or took the blind staggers, or somethin'; there was a lot of tracks. But I give up thinkin' it out, 'cause I knowed if the damn cayuse had jack-rabbited any, Fourteen-foot'd pick him and his load up and carry him. Then I see some wolf tracks — dang near as big as a steer's they was — and I figger Fourteen-foot's had a set-to with a couple of 'em timber cayotes and lammed hell's delight out of 'em, 'cause he could've done it. Then I'm follerin' the cayuse's trail agen, pickin' it up here and there, and all at once it jumps me that the big feet is missin'. Sure I natural figger Johnson's got mussed up a bit with the wolves and is ridin'; but there's the dang wolf tracks agen. And some moccasin feet has been passin' along, too.

Then the hoss tracks cuts out just same's if he'd spread his wings and gone up in the air — they just ain't."

"Then Caribou gets a hunch and goes back and peeks over the cliff." Miner Graham added, for old David had stopped speaking to bit viciously at a black plug of tobacco to hide his feelings.

"I dunno what made me do it," Caribou interrupted; "it was just same's Fourteen-foot's callin' me. There ain't nobody can make me believe that if two men paddles together twenty years, had their little fights, and show-downs, and still sticks, that one of 'em is going to cut clean out just 'cause he goes over the Big Divide — 'tain't natural. I tell you, boys, Fourteen-foot's callin' me — that's what he is, when I goes back."

Then Graham had to take up the narrative, for Caribou, heading straight for the bar, pointed dumbly at a black bottle.

"Yes, Carney," Graham said, "Caribou packs into Buckin' Horse on his back what was left of Fourteen-foot, and there wasn't no gold and no sign of the cayuse. Then we swarms out, a few of us, and picks up cayuse tracks most partic'lar where the Eagle Hills trail hits the trail for Kootenay. And when we overhaul the cayuse that's layin' down 'em tracks it's Fourteen-foot's hawse, and a-ridin' him is Harry Holt."

"And he's got the god you was talkin' 'bout wolves eatin', Bulldog," Kootenay Jim said with a sneer. "He was hangin' 'round here busted, cleaned to the bone, and there he's a-ridin' Fourteen-foot's cayuse, with lots of gold."

"That's the whole case then, is it, boys?" Carney added quietly.

"Ain't it enough?" Kootenay Jim snarled.

"No, it isn't. You were tried for murder once yourself, Kootenay, and you got off, though everybody knew it was the dead man's money in your pocket. You got off because nobody saw you kill the man, and the circumstantial evidence gave you the benefit of the doubt."

"I ain't bein' tried for this, Bulldog. Your bringin' up old scores might get you in wrong."

"You're not being tried, Kootenay, but another man is, and I say he's got to have a fair chance. You bring him here, boys, and let me hear his story; that's only fair, men amongst men. Because I give you fair warning, boys, if this lynching goes through, and you're in wrong, I'm going to denounce you; not one of you will get away — *not one*"

"We'll bring him, Bulldog," Graham said; "what you say is only fair, but swing he will."

Jeanette's brother had been locked in the pen in the log police barracks. He was brought into the Gold Nugget, and his defence was what might be called powerfully weak. It was simply a statement that he had bought the cayuse from an Indian on the trail outside Bucking Horse. He refused to say where he had got the gold, simply declaring that he had killed nobody, had never seen Fourteen-foot Johnson, and knew nothing about the murder.

Something in the earnestness of the man convinced Carney that he was innocent. However, that was, as far as Carney's action was concerned, a minor matter; it was Jeanette's brother, and he was going to save him from being lynched if he had to fight the roomful of men — there was no doubt whatever about that in his mind.

"I can't say, boys," Carney began, "that you can be blamed for thinking you've got the right man."

"That's what we figgered," Graham declared.

"But you've not gone far enough in sifting the evidence if you sure don't want to lynch an innocent man. The only evidence you have is that you caught Harry on Johnson's cayuse. How do you know it's Johnson's cayuse?"

"Caribou says it is," Graham answered.

"And Harry says it was an Indian's cayuse," Carney affirmed.

"He most natural just ordinar'ly lies about it," Kootenay ventured viciously.

"Where's the cayuse?" Carney asked.

"Out in the stable," two or three voices answered.

"I want to see him. Mind, boys, I'm working for you as much as for that poor devil you want to string up, because if you get the wrong man I'm going to denounce you, that's as sure as God made little apples."

His quiet earnestness was compelling. All the fierce heat of passion had gone from the men; there still remained the grim determination that, convinced they were right, nothing but the death of some of them would check. But somehow they felt that the logic of conviction would swing even Carney to their side.

So, without even a word from a leader, they all thronged out to the stable yard; the cayuse was brought forth, and, at Bulldog's request, led up and down the yard, his hoofs leaving an imprint in the bare clay at every step. It was the footprints alone that interested Carney. He studied them intently, a horrible dread in his heart as he searched for that goblined hoof that inturned. But the two forefeet left saucer-like imprints, and, though they were both slightly intoed, as is the way of a cayuse, neither was like the curious goblined track that had so fastened on his fancy out in the Valley of the Grizzley's Bridge.

And also there was the broken toe wall of the hind foot that he had seen on the newer trail.

He turned to Caribou Dave, asking, "What makes you think this is Johnson's pack horse?"

"There ain't no thinkin' 'bout it," Caribou answered with asperity. "When I see my boots I don't *think* they're mine, I just most natur'ly figger they are and pull 'em on. I'd know that dun-coloured rat if I see him in a wild herd."

"And yet," Carney objected in an even tone, "this isn't the cayuse that Johnson toted out his duffel from the Eagle Hills on."

A cackle issued from Kootenay Jim's long, scraggy neck:

"That settles it boys; Bulldog passes the buck and the game's over. Caribou is just an ord'nary liar, 'cordin' to Judge Carney.

"Caribou is perfectly honest in his belief," Carney declared. "There isn't more than half a dozen colours for horses, and there are a good many thousand horses in this territory, so a great many of them are the same Collor. And the general structure of different cayuses is as similar as so many wheelbarrows. That brand on his shoulder may be a C, or a new moon, or a flapjack."

He turned to Caribou: "What brand had Fourteen-foot's cayuse?"

"I don't know," the old chap answered surlily, "but it was there same place it's restin' now — it ain't shifted none since you fingered it."

"That won't do, boys," Carney said; "if Caribou can't swear to a horse's brand, how can he swear to the beast?"

"And if Fourteen-foot'd come back and stand up here and swear it was his hawse, that wouldn't do either, would it, Bulldog?" And Kootenay cackled.

"Johnson wouldn't say so — he'd know better. His cayuse had a club foot, an inturned left forefoot. I picked it up, here and there, for miles back on the trail, sometimes fair on top of Johnson's big boot track, and sometimes Johnson's were on top when he travelled behind.

The men stared; and Graham asked: "What do you say to that, Caribou? Did you ever map out Fourteen-foot's cayuse — what his travellers was like?"

"I never looked at his feet — there wasn't no reason to; I was minin'."

"There's another little test we can make," Carney suggested. "Have you got any of Johnson's belongings — a coat?"

"We got his coat," Graham answered; "it was pretty bad wrecked with the wolves, and we kinder fixed the remains up decent in a suit of store clothes."

At Carney's request the coat was brought, a rough Mackinaw, and from one of the men present he got a miner's magnifying glass, saying, as he examined the coat:

"This ought, naturally, to be pretty well filled with hairs from that cayuse of Johnson's; and while two horses may look alike, there's generally a difference in the hair."

Carney's surmise proved correct; dozens of short hairs were imbedded in the coat, principally in the sleeves. Then hair was plucked from many difference parts of the cayuse's body, and the two lots were viewed through the glass. They were different. The hair on the cayuse standing in the yard was coarser, redder, longer, for its Indian owner had let it run like a wild goat; and Fourteen-foot had given his cayuse considerable attention. There were also some white hairs in the coat warp, and on this cayuse there was not a single white hair to be seen.

When questioned Caribou would not emphatically declare that there had not been a star or a white stripe in the forehead of Johnson's horse.

These things caused one or two of the men to waver, for if it were not Johnson's cayuse, if Caribou were mistaken, there was no direct evidence to connect Harry Holt with the murder.

Kootenay Jim objected that the examination of the hair was nothing; that Carney, like a clever lawyer, was trying to get the murderer off on a technicality. As to the club foot they had only Carney's guess, whereas Caribou had never seen any club foot on Johnson's horse.

"We can prove that part of it." Graham said; "we can go back on the trail and see what Bulldog seen."

Half a dozen men approved this, saying: "We'll put off the hangin' and go back."

But Carney objected.

When he did so Kootenay Jim and John from Slocan raised a howl of derision, Kootenay saying: "When we calls his bluff he throws his hand in the discard. There ain't no club foot anywhere; it's just a game to gain time to give this coyote, Holt, a chance to make a get-away. We're being' buffaloed — we're wastin' time. We gets a murderer on a murdered man's hawse, with the gold in his pockets, and Bulldog Carney puts some hawse hairs under a glass, hands out a pipe dream 'bout some ghost tracks back on the trail, and reaches out to grab the pot. Hell! you'd think we was a damn lot of tenderfeet."

This harangue had an effect on the angry men, but seemingly none whatever upon Bulldog, for he said quietly:

"I don't want a troop of men to go back on the trail just now, because I'm going out myself to bring the murderer in. I can get him alone, for if he does see me he won't think that I'm after him, simply that I'm trailing. But if a party goes they'll never see him. He's a clever devil and will make his get-away. All I want on this evidence is that you hold Holt till I get back. I'll bring the foreleg of that cayuse with a club foot, for there's no doubt the murderer made sure that the wolves got him too."

They had worked back into the hotel by now, and, inside, Kootenay Jim and his two cronies had each taken a big drink of whisky, whispering together as they drank.

As Carney and Graham entered, Kootenay's shrill voice was saying:

"We're bein' flim-flammed — played for a lot of kids. There ain't been a damn thing 'cept lookin' at some hawse hairs through a glass. Men has been murdered on the trail, and who done it — somebody. Caribou's mate was murdered, and we find his gold on a man that was stony broke here, was bummin' on the town, spongin' on Seth Long; he hadn't two bits. And 'cause his sister stands well with Bulldog he palms this three-card trick with hawse hairs, and we got to let the murderer go."

"You lie Kootenay!" The words had come from Jeanette. "My brother wouldn't tell you where he got the gold — he'd let you hang him first; but I will tell. I took it out of Seth's safe and gave it to him to get out of the country, because I knew that you and those two other hounds, Slocan and Denver, would murder him some night because he knocked you down for insulting me."

"That's a lie!" Kootenay screamed; "you and Bulldog 're runnin' mates and you've put this up."

There was a cry of warning from Slocan, and Kootenay whirled, drawing his gun. As he did so his arm dropped and his gun clattered to the floor, for Carney's bullet had splintered its butt, incidentally clipping away a finger. And the same weapon in Carney's hand was covering Slocan and Denver as they stood side by side, their backs to the bar.

No one spoke; almost absolute stillness hung in the air for five seconds. Half the men in the room had drawn, but no one pulled a trigger — no one spoke.

It was Carney who broke the silence:

"Jeanette, bind that hound's hand up; and you, Seth, send for the doctor — I guess he's too much of a man to be in this gang."

A wave of relief swept over the room; men coughed or spat as the tension slipped, dropping their guns back into holsters.

Kootenay Jim, cowed by the damaged hand, holding it in his left, followed Jeanette out of the room.

As the girl disappeared Harry Holt, who had stood between the two men, his wrists bound behind his back said:

"My sister told a lie to shield me. I stole the gold myself from Seth's safe. I wanted to get out of this hell hole 'cause I knew I'd got to kill Kootenay or he'd get me. That's why I didn't 'ell before where the gold come from."

"Here, Seth," Carney called as Long came back into the room, "you missed any gold — what do you know about Holt's story that he got the gold from your safe?"

"I ain't looked — I don't keep no close track of what's in that iron box; I jus' keep the key, and a couple of bags might get lifted and I wouldn't know. If Jeanette took a bag or two to stake her brother, I guess she's got a right to, 'cause we're pardners in all I got."

"I took the key when Seth was sleeping," Harry declared. "Jeanette didn't know I was going to take it."

"But your sister claims she took it, so how'd she say that if it ain't a frame-up?" Graham asked.

"I told her just as I was pullin' out, so she wouldn't let Seth get in wrong by blamin' her or somebody else."

"Don't you see, boys," Carney interposed, "if you'd swung off this man, and all this was proved afterwards, you'd be in wrong? You didn't find on Harry a tenth of the gold Fourteen-foot likely had."

"That skunk hid it," Caribou declared; "he just kept enough to get out with."

Poor old Caribou was thirsting for revenge; in his narrowed hate he would have been satisfied if the party had pulled a perfect stranger off a passenger train and lynched him; it would have been a *quid pro quo*. He felt that he was being cheated by the superior cleverness of Bulldog Carney. He had seen miners beaten out of their just gold claims by professional sharks; the fine reasoning, the microscopic evidence of the hairs, the intoed hoof, all these things were beyond him. He was honest in his conviction that the cayuse was Johnson's, and feared that the man who had killed his friend would slip through their fingers.

"It's just like this, boys," he said, "me and Fourteen-foot was together so long that if he was away somewhere I'd know he was comin' back a day afore he hit camp — I'd feel it, same's I turned back on the trail there and found him all chawed up by the wolves. There wasn't no reason to look over that cliff only ol' Fourteen-foot a-callin' me. And now he's a-tellin' me inside that that skunk there murdered him when he wasn't lookin'. And if you chaps ain't got the sand to push this to a finish I'll get the man that killed Fourteen-foot; he won't never get away. If you boys is just a pack of coyotes that howls good and plenty till somebody calls 'em, and is goin' to slink with your tails between your legs for fear you'll be rounded up for the lynchin', you can turn this murderer loose right now — you don't need to worry what'll happen to him. I'll be too danged lonesome without Fourteen-foot to figger what's comin' to me. Turn him loose — take the hobbles off him. You fellers go home and pull your blankets over your heads so's you won't see no ghosts."

Carney's sharp gray eyes watched the old fanatic's very move; he let him talk till he had exhausted himself with his passionate words; then he said:

"Caribou, you're some man. You'd go through a whole tribe of Indians for a chum. You believe you're right, and that's just what I'm trying to do in this, find out who is right — we don't want to wrong anybody. You can come back on the trail with me, and I'll show you the club-footed tracks; I'll let you help me get the right man."

The old chap turned his humpy shoulders, and looked at Carney out of bleary, weasel eyes set beneath shaggy brows; then he shrilled:

"I'll see you in hell fust; I've heerd o' you, Bulldog; I've heerd you had a wolverine skinned seven ways of the jack for tricks, and by the rings on a Big Horn I believe it. You know that while I'm here that jack rabbit ain't goin' to get away — and he ain't; you can bet your soul on that, Bulldog. We'd go out on the trail and we'd find that Wiesah-ke-chack, the Indian's devil, had stole 'em pipedream, club-footed tracks, and when we come back the man that killed my chum, old Fourteen-foot, would be down somewhere where a smart-Aleck lawyer 'd get him off."

It took an hour of cool reasoning on the part of Carney to extract from that roomful of men a promise that they would give Holt three days of respite, Carney giving his word that he would not send out any information to the police but would devote the time to bringing in the murderer.

Kootenay Jim had had his wound dressed. He was in an ugly mood over the shooting, but the saner members of the lynching party felt that he had brought the quarrel on himself; that he had turned so viciously on Jeanette, whom they all liked, caused the men to feel that he had got pretty much his just desserts. He had drawn his gun first, and when a man does that he's got to take the consequences. He was a gambler, and a gambler generally had to abide by the gambling chance in gun play as well as by the fall of a card.

But Carney had work to do, and he was just brave enough not to be foolhardy. He knew that the three toughs would waylay him in the dark without compunction. They were now thirsting not only for young Holt's life, but his. So, saying openly that he would start in the morning, when it was dark he slipped through the back entrance of the hotel to the stable, and led his buckskin out through a corral and by a back way to the tunnel entrance of the abandoned Little Widow mine. Here he left the horse and returned to the hotel, set up the drinks, and loafed about for a time, generally giving the three desperadoes the impression that he was camped for the night in the Gold Nugget, though Graham, in whom he had confided, knew different.

Presently he slipped away, and Jeanette, who had got the key from Seth, unlocked the door that led down to the long communicating drift, at the other end of which was the opening to the Little Widow mine.

Jeanette closed the door and followed Carney down the stairway. At the foot of the stairs he turned, saying: "You shouldn't do this."

"Why, Bulldog?"

"Well, you saw why this afternoon. Kootenay Jim has got an arm in a sling because he can't understand. Men as a rule don't understand much about women, so a woman has always got to wear armour."

"But we understand, Bulldog; and Seth does."

"Yes, girl, we understand; but Seth can only understand the evident. You clamber up the stairs quick."

"My God! Bulldog, see what you're doing for me now. You never would stand for Harry yourself."

"If he'd been my brother I should, just as you have, girl."

"That's it, Bulldog, you're doing all this, standing there holding up a mob of angry men, because he's *my* brother."

"You called the turn, Jeanette."

"And all I can do, all I can say is, *thank you*. Is that all?"

"That's all, girl. It's more than enough."

He put a strong hand on her arm, almost shook her, saying with an earnestness that the playful tone hardly masked:

"When you've got a true friend let him do all the friending — then you'll hold him; the minute you try to rearrange his life you start backing the losing card. Now, good-bye, girl; I've got work to do. I'll bring in that wolf of the trail; I've got him marked down in a cave — I'll get him. You tell that pin-headed brother of yours to stand pat. And if Kootenay starts any deviltry go straight to Graham. Good-bye."

Cool fingers touched the girl on the forehead; then she stood alone watching the figure slipping down the gloomed passage of the drift, lighted candle in hand.

Carney led his buckskin from the mine tunnel, climbed the hillside to a back trail, and mounting, rode silently at a walk till the yellow blobs of light that was Bucking Horse lay behind him. Then at a little hunch of his heels the horse broke into a shuffling trot.

It was near midnight when he camped; both he and the buckskin had eaten robustly back at the Gold Nugget Hotel, and Carney, making the horse lie down by tapping him gently on the shins with his quirt, rolled himself in his blanket and slept close beside the buckskin — they were like two men in a huge bed.

All next day he rode, stopping twice to let the buckskin feed, and eating a dry meal himself, building no fire. He had a conviction that the murderer of the gold hunters made the Valley of the Grizzley's Bridge his stalking ground. And if the devil who stalked these returning miners was still there he felt certain that he would get him.

There had been nothing to rouse the murderer's suspicion that these men were known to have been murdered.

A sort of fatality hangs over a man who once starts in on a crime of that sort; he becomes like a man who handles dynamite — careless, possessed of a sense of security, of fatalism. Carney had found all desperadoes that way, each murder had made them more sure of themselves, it generally had been so easy.

Caribou Dave had probably passed without being seen by the murderer; indeed he had passed that point early in the morning, probably while the ghoul of the trail slept; the murderer would reason that if there was any suspicion in Bucking Horse that miners had been made away with, a posse would have come riding over the back trail, and the murderer would have ample knowledge of their approach.

To a depraved mind, such as his, there was a terrible fascination in this killing of men, and capturing their gold; he would keep at it like a gambler who has struck a big winning streak; he would pile up gold, probably in the cave Carney had seen the mouth of, even if it were more than he could take away. It was the curse of the lust of gold, and, once started, the devilish murder lust.

Carney had an advantage. He was looking for a man in a certain locality, and the man, not knowing of his approach, not dreading it, would be watching the trail in the other direction for victims. Even if he had met him full on the trail Carney would have passed the time of day and ridden on, as if going up into the Eagle Hills. And no doubt the murderer would let him pass without action. It was only returning miners he was interested in. Yes, Carney had an advantage, and if the man were still there he would get him.

His plan was to ride the buckskin to within a short distance of where the murders had been committed, which was evidently in the neighbourhood of the cliff at the bottom of which Fourteen-foot Johnson had been found, and go forward on foot until he had thoroughly reconnoitred the ground. He felt that he would catch sight of the murderer somewhere between that point and the cave, for he was convinced that the cave was the home of this trail devil.

The uncanny event of the wolves was not so simple. The curious tone of the wolf's howl had suggested a wild dog — that is, a creature that was half dog, half wolf; either whelped that way in the forests, or a train dog that had escaped. Even a fanciful weird thought entered Carney's mind that the murderer might be on terms of dominion over this half-wild pair; they might know him well enough to leave him alone, and yet devour his victims. This was conjecture, rather far-fetched, but still not impossible. An Indian's train dogs would obey their master, but pull down a white man quick enough if he were helpless.

However, the man was the thing.

The sun was dipping behind the jagged fringe of mountaintops to the west when Carney slipped down into the Valley of the Grizzley's Bridge, and, fording the stream, rode on to within a hundred and fifty yards of the spot where his buckskin had shied from the trail two days before.

Dismounting, he took off his coat and draping it over the horse's neck said: "Now you're anchored, Patsy — stand steady."

Then he unbuckled the snaffle bit and rein from the bridle and wound the rein about his waist. Carney knew that the horse, not hampered by a dangling rein to catch in his legs or be seized by a man, would protect himself. No man but Carney could saddle the buckskin or mount him unless he was roped or thrown; and his hind feet were as deft as the fists of a boxer.

Then he moved steadily along the trail, finding here and there the imprint of moccasined feet that had passed over the trail since he had. There were the fresh pugs of two wolves, the dog-wolf's paws enormous.

Carney's idea was to examine closely the trail that ran by the cliff to where his horse had shied from the path in the hope of finding perhaps the evidences of struggle, patches of blood soaked into the brown earth, and then pass on to where he could command a view of the cave mouth. If the murderer had his habitat there he would be almost certain to show himself at that hour, either returning from up the trail where he might have been on the lookout for approaching victims, or to issue from the cave for water or firewood for his evening meal. Just what he should do Carney had not quite determined. First he would stalk the man in hopes of finding out something that was conclusive.

If the murderer were hiding in the cave the gold would almost certainly be there.

That was the order of events, so to speak, when Carney, hand

on gun, and eyes fixed ahead on the trail, came to the spot where
the wolf had stood at bay. The trail took a twist, a projecting rock
bellied it into a little turn, and a fallen birch lay across it, half
smothered in a lake of leaves and brush.

As Carney stepped over the birch there was a crashing clamp of
iron, and the powerful jaws of a bear trap closed on his leg with such
numbing force that he almost went out. His brain swirled; there
were roaring noises in his head, an excruciating grind on his leg.

His senses steadying, his first cogent thought was that the bone
was smashed; but a limb of the birch, caught in the jaws, squelched
to splinters, had saved the bone; this and his breeches and heavy
socks in the legs of his strong riding boots.

As if the snapping steel had carried down the valley, the
evening stillness was rent by the yelping howl of a wolf beyond
where the cave hung on the hillside. There was something
demoniac in this, suggesting to the half-dazed man that the wolf
stood as sentry.

The utter helplessness of his position came to him with dull
force; he could no more open the jaws of that double-springed trap
than he could crash the door of a safe. And a glance showed him
that the trap was fastened to a piece of loose log.

The fiendish deviltry of the man who had set it was evident.
The whole vile scheme flashed upon Carney; it was set where the
trail narrowed before it wound down to the gorge, and the man
caught in it could be killed by a club, or left to be devoured by the
wolves. A pistol might protect him for a little short time against the
wolves, but that even could be easily wheedled out of a man caught
by the murderer coming with a pretense of helping him.

Suddenly a voice fell on Carney's ear:

"Throw your gun out on the trail in front of you! I've got you
covered, Bulldog, and you haven't got a chance on earth."

Now Carney could make out a pistol, a man's head, and a
crooked arm projecting from beside a tree twenty yards along the
trail.

"Throw out the gun, and I'll parley with you!" the voice added.

Carney recognized the voice as that of Jack the Wolf, and he
knew that the offered parley was only a blind, a trick to get his gun
away so that he would be a quick victim for the wolves; that would
save a shooting. Sometimes an imbedded bullet told the absolute
tale of murder.

"There's nothing doing in that line, Jack the Wolf," Carney answered; "you can shoot and be damned to you! I'd rather die that way than be torn to pieces by the wolves."

Jack the Wolf seemed to debate this matter behind the tree; then he said: "It's your own fault if you get into my bear trap, Bulldog; I ain't invited you in. I've been watchin' you for the last hour, and I've been a-wonderin' just what your little game was. Me and you ain't good 'nough friends for me to step up there to help you out, and you got a gun on you. You throw it out and I'll parley. If you'll agree to certain things, I'll spring that trap, and you can ride away, 'cause I guess you'll keep your word. I don't want to kill nobody, I don't."

The argument was specious. If Carney had not known Jack the Wolf as absolutely bloodthirsty, he might have taken a chance and thrown the gun.

"You know perfectly well, Jack the Wolf, that if you came to help me out, and I shot you, I'd be committing suicide, so you're lying."

"You mean you won't give up the gun?"

"No."

"Well, keep it, damn you! Them wolves knows a thing or two. One of 'em knows pretty near as much about guns as you do. They'll just sit off there in the dark and laugh at you till you drop; then you'll never wake up. You think it over, Bulldog, I'm —"

The speaker's voice was drowned by the howl of the wolf a short distance down the valley.

"D'you hear him, Bulldog?" Jack queried when the howls had died down. "They get your number on the wind and they're sayin' you're their meat. You think over my proposition while I go down and gather in your buckskin; he looks good to me for a get-away. You let me know when I come back what you'll do, 'cause 'em wolves is in a hurry — they're hungry; and I guess your leg ain't none too comf'table."

Then there was silence, and Carney knew that Jack the Wolf was circling through the bush to where his horse stood, keeping out of range as he travelled.

Carney knew that the buckskin would put up a fight; his instinct would tell him that Jack the Wolf was evil. The howling wolf would also have raised the horse's mettle; but he himself was in the awkward position of being a loser, whether man or horse won.

From where he was trapped the buckskin was in view. Carney saw his head go up, the lop-ears throw forward in rigid listening, and he could see, beyond, off to the right, the skulking form of Jack slipping from tree to tree so as to keep the buckskin between him and Carney.

Now the horse turned his arched neck and snorted. Carney whipped out his gun, a double purpose in his mind. If Jack the Wolf offered a fair mark he would try a shot, though at a hundred and fifty yards it would be a chance; and he must harbour his cartridges for the wolves; the second purpose was that the shot would rouse the buckskin with a knowledge that there was a battle on.

Jack the Wolf came to the trail beyond the horse and was now slowly approaching, speaking in coaxing terms. The horse, warily alert, was shaking his head; then he pawed at the earth like an angry bull.

Ten yards from the horse Jack stood still, his eye noticing that the bridle rein and bit were missing. Carney saw him uncoil from his waist an ordinary packing rope; it was not a lariat, being short. With this in a hand held behind his back, Jack, with short steps, moved slowly toward the buckskin, trying to soothe the wary animal with soft speech.

Ten feet from the horse he stood again, and Carney knew what that meant — a little quick dash in to twist the rope about the horse's head, or seize him by the nostrils. Also the buckskin knew. He turned his rump to the man, threw back his ears, and lashed out with his hind feet as a warning to the horse thief. The coat had slipped from his neck to the ground.

Jack the Wolf tried circling tactics, trying to gentle the horse into a sense or security with soothing words. Once, thinking he had a chance, he sprang for the horse's head, only to escape those lightning heels by the narrowest margin; at that instant Carney fired, but his bullet missed, and Jack, startled, stood back, planning sulkily.

Carney saw him thread out his rope with the noose end in his right hand, and circle again. Then the hand with a half-circle sent the loop swishing through the air, and at the first cast it went over the buckskin's head.

Carney had been waiting for this. He whistled shrilly the signal that always brought the buckskin to his side.

Jack had started to work his way up the rope, hand over hand, but at the well-known signal the horse whirled, the rope slipped through Jack's sweaty hands, a loop of it caught his leg, and he was thrown. The buckskin, strung to a high nervous tension, answered his master's signal at a gallop, and the rope, fastened to Jack's waist, dragged him as though he hung from a runaway horse with a foot in the stirrup. His body struck rocks, trees, roots; it jiggered about on the rough earth like a cork, for the noose had slipped back to the buckskin's shoulders.

Just as the horse reached Carney, Jack the Wolf's two legs straddled a slim tree and the body wedged there. Carney snapped his fingers, but as the horse stepped forward the rope tightened, the body was fast.

"Damned if I want to tear the cuss to pieces, Patsy," he said, drawing forth his pocket knife. He just managed by reaching out with his long arm, to cut the rope, and the horse thrust his velvet muzzle against his master's cheek, as if he would say, "Now, old pal, we're all right — don't worry."

Bulldog understood the reassurance and, patting the broad wise forehead, answered: "We can play the wolves together, Pat — I'm glad you're here. It's a hundred to one on us yet." Then a half-smothered oath startled the horse, for, at a twist, a shoot of agony raced along the vibrant nerves to Carney's brain.

In the subsidence of strife Carney was cognizant of the night shadows that had crept along the valley; it would soon be dark. Perhaps he could build a little fire; it would keep the wolves at bay, for in the darkness they would come; it would give him a circle of light, and a target when the light fell on their snarling faces.

Bending gingerly down he found in the big bed of leaves a network of dead branches that Jack the Wolf had cunningly placed there to hold the leaves. There was within reach on the dead birch some of its silver parchment-like bark. With his cowboy hat he brushed the leaves away from about his limbs, then taking off his belt he lowered himself gingerly to his free knee and built a little mound of sticks and bark against the birch log. Then he put his hand in a pocket for matches — every pocket; he had not one match; they were in his coat lying down somewhere on the trail. He looked longingly at the body lying wedged against the tree; Jack would have matches, for no man travelled the wilds without the means to a fire. But matches in New York were about as accessible as any that might be in the dead man's pockets.

Philosophic thought with one leg in a bear trap is practically impossible, and Carney's arraignment of tantalizing Fate, or something, cast into the trapped man's mind a magical inspiration — a vital grievance. His mind, acute because of his dilemma and pain, must have wandered far ahead of his cognizance, for a sane plan of escape lay evident. If he had a fire he could heat the steel springs of that trap. The leaves of the spring were thin, depending upon that elusive quality, the steel's temper, for strength. If he could heat the steel, even to a dull red, the temper would leave it as a spirit forsakes a body, and the spring would bend like cardboard.

"And I haven't got a damn match," Carney wailed. Then he looked at the body. "But you've got them —"

He grasped the buckskin's headpiece and drew him forward a pace; then he unslung his picket line and made a throw for Jack the Wolf's head. If he could yank the body around, the wedged legs would clear.

Throwing a lariat at a man lying groggily flat, with one of the thrower's legs in a bear trap, was a new one on Carney — it was some test.

Once he muttered grimly, from between set teeth: "If my leg holds out I'll get him yet, Patsy."

Then he threw the lariat again, only to drag the noose hopelessly off the head that seemed glued to the ground, the dim light blurring form and earth into a shadow from which thrust, indistinctly, the pale face that carried a crimson mark from forehead to chin.

He had made a dozen casts, all futile, the noose sometimes catching slightly at the shaggy head, even causing it to roll weirdly, as if the man were not dead but dodging the rope. As Carney slid the noose from his hand to float gracefully out toward the body his eye caught the dim form of the dog-wolf, just beyond, his slobbering jaws parted, giving him the grinning aspect of a laughing hyena. Carney snatched the rope and dropped his hand to his gun, but the wolf was quicker than the man — he was gone. A curious thing had happened, though, for that erratic twist of the rope had spiralled the noose beneath Jack the Wolf's chin, and gently, vibratingly tightening the slip, Carney found it hold. Then, hand over hand, he hauled the body to the birch log, and, without ceremony, searched it for matches. He found them, wrapped in an oilskin in a pocket of Jack's shirt. He noticed, casually, that Jack's gun had been torn from its belt during the owner's rough voyage.

The finding of the matches was like an anaesthetic to the agony of the clamp on his leg. He chuckled, saying, "Patsy, it's a million to one on us; they can't beat us, old pard."

He transferred his faggots and birch bark to the loops of the springs, one pile at either end of the trap, and touched a match to them.

The acrid smoke almost stifled him; sparks burnt his hands, and his wrists, and his face; the jaws of the trap commenced to catch the heat as it travelled along the conducting steel, and he was threatened with the fact that he might burn his leg off. With his knife he dug up the black moist earth beneath the leaves, and dribbled it on to the heating jaws.

Carney was so intent on his manifold duties that he had practically forgotten Jack the Wolf; but as he turned his face from an inspection of a spring that was reddening, he saw a pair of black vicious eyes watching him, and a hand reaching for his gun belt that lay across the birch log.

The hands of both men grasped the belt at the same moment, and a terrible struggle ensued. Carney was handicapped by the trap, which seemed to bite into his leg as if it were one of the wolves fighting Jack's battle; and Jack the Wolf showed, by his vain efforts to rise, that his legs had been made almost useless in that drag by the horse.

Carney had in one hand a stout stick with which he had been adjusting his fire, and he brought this down on the other's wrist, almost shattering the bone. With a cry of pain Jack the Wolf released his grasp of the belt, and Carney, pulling the gun, covered him, saying:

"Hoped you were dead, Jack the Murderer! Now turn face down on this log, with your hands behind your back, till I hobble you."

"I can spring that trap with a lever and let you out," Jack offered.

"Don't need you — I'm going to see you hanged and don't want to be under any obligation to you, murderer; turn over quick or I'll kill you now — my leg is on fire."

Jack the Wolf knew that a man with a bear trap on his leg, and a gun in his hand, was not a man to trifle with, so he obeyed.

When Jack's wrists were tied with the picket line, Carney took a loop about the prisoner's legs; then he turned to his fires.

The struggle had turned the steel springs from the fires; but in the twisting one of them had been bent so that its spring had slipped down from the jaws. Now Carney heaped both fires under the other spring and soon it was so hot that, when balancing his weight on the leg in the trap, he place his other foot on it and shifted his weight, the strip of steel went down like paper. He was free.

At first Carney could not bear the weight on the mangled leg; it felt as if it had been asleep for ages; the blood rushing through the released veins pricked like a tattooing needle. He took off his boot and massaged the limb, Jack eyeing this proceeding sardonically. The two wolves hovered beyond the firelight, snuffling and yapping.

When he could hobble on the injured limb Carney put the bit and bridle rein back on the buckskin, and turning to Jack, unwound the picket line from his legs, saying, "Get up and lead the way to that cave!"

"I can't walk, Bulldog," Jack protested; "my leg's half broke."

"Take your choice — get on your legs, or I'll tie you up and leave you for the wolves," Carney snapped.

Jack the Wolf knew his Bulldog Carney well. As he rose groggily to his feet, Carney lifted the saddle, holding the loose end of the picket line that was fastened to Jack's wrists, and said:

"Go on in front; if you try any tricks I'll put a bullet through you — this sore leg's got me peeved."

At the cave Carney found, as he expected, several little canvas bags of gold, and other odds and ends such as a murderer too often, and also foolishly, will garner from his victims. But he also found something he had not expected to find — the cayuse that had belonged to Fourteen-foot Johnson, for Jack the Wolf had preserved the cayuse to pack out his wealth.

Next morning, no chance of action having come to Jack the Wolf through the night, for he had lain tied up like a turkey that is to be roasted, he started on the pilgrimage to Bucking Horse, astride Fourteen-foot Johnson's cayuse, with both feet tied beneath that sombre animal's belly. Carney landed him and the gold in that astonished berg.

And in the fullness of time something very serious happened to the enterprising man of the bear trap.

This page intentionally left blank

A TALE OF THE GRAND JARDIN

by W.H. Blake
from *Brown Waters and Other Sketches*. Toronto: Macmillan
Company of Canada, 1915.

Who knows what horrors lurk in the wilderness of the Canadian Shield.
The Native peoples knew and feared the cannibal spirit they called the
Wendigo.

This page intentionally left blank

H is story comes back to me in sharp and vivid outline, though I look across years not a few to the telling of it, and to our little tent pitched high and lonely in the Grand Jardin des Ours. Who can say what share time and place, the wild August storm, and my friend's emotion, had in etching the picture so deeply on my memory? Perhaps the impression is not communicable; perhaps it may be caught, if you will consent to make camp with us in those great barrens that lie far-stretching and desolate among the Laurentian Mountains.

We had been fishing the upper reaches of one of the little rivers that rise in the heart of the hills, quickly gather volume from many streams and lakes, loiter for a few miles in dead waters where a canoe will float, through amazing gorges, to the St. Lawrence and the sea. An evening rare and memorable, when the great trout were mad for the fly; more than a dozen of these splendid fellows, a man's full load, lay on the bank, where they rivalled the autumn foliage in crimson, orange, and bronze. This first good luck came after many barren days, the smoke-house of bark was still unfilled — so it happened that we did not leave the river till the darkness, and the thunder of an oncoming storm put down the fish. From the towering cumulus that overhung us immense drops plumped into the water-like pebbles, and the steady roar of the advancing squall warned us to hasten. Gathering up the trout we dashed for the tent, to find it will nigh beaten to the ground by the weight of the wind and the rain. Though a clump of stunted spruces to windward gave a little shelter, we had much ado to keep the friendly canvas roof over our heads by anchoring it with stones.

After putting on dry clothes we explored the provision sack, discovering nothing more inviting that pork and crumbled biscuit. Tea there was, but even an old hand could not boil a kettle, or cook fish, in such a tumult of rain and wind. Three weeks of wandering had brought us to the lowest ebb, and our men, who had departed in the morning for an outpost of civilization where supplies could be obtained, would scarcely return in such weather. We guessed, and rightly as it turned out, that they had chosen to spend the night at La Galette, the nerve-extremity, responding faintly to impulses from the world of men, where the gossip of the countryside awaited them.

So were we two alone in one of the loneliest places this wide earth knows. Mile upon mile of gray moss; weathered granite clad in ash-coloured lichen; old *brûlé* — the trees here fallen in windrows, there standing bleached and lifeless, making the hilltops look barer, like the sparse white hairs of age. Only in the gullies a little greenness — dwarfed larches, gnarled birches, tiny firs a hundred years old — and always moss, softer than Persian rug — moss to the ankle, moss to the knee, great boulders covered with it, the very quagmires mossed over so that a careless step plunges one into the sucking black ooze below.

Through the door of the tent the lightning showed this endless desolation, and a glimpse of the river forcing its angry way through a defile.

When the sorry meal was over we smoked, by turns supporting the tent pole in the heavier gusts. My companion was absent-minded and restless; he seemed to have no heart for the small talk of the woods, and to be listening for something. Breaking into an attempt of mine at conversation, he asked abruptly:

"Did you ever hear about the disappearance of Paul Duchêne?"

The name came back to me in a misty way, and with some tragic association, but the man himself I had never known. Any sort of a yarn was welcome that would take one's mind off the eeriness and discomfort of our situation, and H_____ required no urging. He spoke like a man who has a tale that must be told, and I try to give you neither more nor less than what he said:

"Duchêne was in camp with me years ago, in fact it was he that brought me into this country in the old days before trails were cut, and when no one came here but himself and his brothers, and a few wandering Montagnais Indians. The Duchênes were trappers, and they guarded the secrets of the place very jealously, which was natural enough as it yielded them game and fur in plenty. Though he showed me good sport, it was quite plain that he never told all that he knew. The paths he followed, if indeed they were paths, were not blazed. He seemed to steer by a sense of direction, and from a general knowledge of the lie of the mountains, valleys, and rivers. Seldom did we return by the way that had taken us to the feeding grounds of moose or caribou. Duchêne was contemptuous of easy walking, and almost seemed to choose the roughest going, but he jogged along in marvellous fashion through swamps and windfalls, with a cruel load on his back. The fellow was simply hard as nails, and, measured by my abilities, was tireless.

"Looking back to that autumn, it strikes me that there was something demonic in his energy. Food and rest did not matter to him. He was always ready to go anywhere — leaving me to follow as best I could; and though I was a pretty stout walker, and carried but little compared to him, it was only shame that kept me from begging for mercy on the long portages.

"Only a few weeks after our trip together Duchêne went out of his mind, and took to the woods. For ten days he wandered in the mountains without food, gun, or matches, but he appears to have partially regained his senses, and made for La Galette, where he arrived in a very distressing condition. Under his father's roof he fell into a harmless, half-witted existence, which lasted for several months. With the spring the fit came upon him again and he disappeared. The brothers followed his trail for days, but lost it finally in the valley of the Enfer, nor were they ever able to discover further trace of him. No man knows what end he made, nor where in this great wilderness his bones are bleaching.

"You have heard, perhaps, the belief of the Montagnais —

strange medley of Paganism and Christianity, that those who die insane without the blessing of a priest become wendigos — werewolves, with nothing human but the their form, soulless beings of a diabolic strength and cunning, that wander for all time seeking only to harm whomever comes their way. A black superstitious race these Indians are, and horribly sincere in their faith. They shot down a young girl with the beads of her rosary, because her mind was weakening, and they thought thus to avert the fate from her, and themselves. You would not doubt the truth of this, had you seen the look in the eyes of the man who told me that he had been a helpless witness of the murder.

"I have never spoken of what happened to me the following summer, because one does not like to be disbelieved; perhaps tonight, with the storm-hags abroad and the voices of the sky filling our ears, you will understand. Our tent is pitched so near that infernal spot, — the whole thing takes possession of me again. I keep listening —

"You know the Rivière à l'Enfer, but you have not seen its headwaters, and never will if you are wise. A queer lot of tales old and new, but all pointing to prodigious trout, took me past the mouth of the canyon that gives the river its name. A bold man might follow this cleft in the mountain, but he would go in peril of his life; the precipitous ascent on the left side is safer, if not easier.

"Duchêne would not guide me there, but he gave an extraordinary account of the fishing in the lake which is the source of the river. There is an Indian tradition, and these traditions usually have a foundation of some kind, that it contains trout of tremendous size. Duchêne asserted that stout lines he had set through the ice, in the morning were found broken. Trying again, with the heaviest gear, his tackle was smashed as easily. Heaven knows what the lake holds; nothing came to my fly but half a dozen ink-black trout a few inches long.

"Very little over a hundred years ago it was firmly believed that an active volcano existed not far from here, and this lake, at the very summit of one of the hills to the northwest of us, fills to the brim what looks like an old crater.

"The good fellows who were with me did not seem to like this fancy of mine to push to the source of the stream, but I cannot say whether this was due to the uncanny reputation of the place, or to the fact that we had nothing but Duchêne's vague description, and the flow of the water to guide us. It was a heavy task to get a canoe up to the lake through that difficult country, and it is very safe to say that mine was the first craft ever launched on its gloomy surface.

"I began fishing at once, but nothing stirred; this was what one might expect in water without a ripple, beneath a cloudless sky; there could be no fair trial under such conditions, before the time of the evening rise. I made some soundings, but my two lines together did not fetch bottom a hundred feet from the shore. The slope under water is very steep, and huge fragments of stone hanging there, seem ready, at a touch, to plunge into the depths. It is hard to describe the colour of the water; like neither the clear brown of the river we fished today, nor the opaque blackness of the swamp rivulets; transparent ink comes nearest to it.

"No stream feeds the lake, but there must be powerful springs below, for the *décharge* flows strongly through a channel of boulders, with water weed moving in the current like something snaky and alive. The tent was pitched on a patch of black sand at the farther shore, the only level spot we could find, and, climbing a few feet higher, I looked out over the bleakest prospect of crag and valley, of moss and granite, till the eye met and welcomed the line of the horizon, and the blue above. Beside me three dead whitened firs, the height of a man, were held in a cleft of the rock, and some fantastic turn of the mind made of the place a wild and dreary Cavalry.

"The sea is old and the wind is old, but they are also eternally young. Of the elements it is only earth that speaks of the never-hastening, never-resting passage from life to death — where the years of a man are an unregarded moment in the march of all things toward that end which may be the beginning. Here on this peak of the world's most ancient hills it seemed to me as though creation had long passed the flood, and was ebbing to its final low tide.

"There fell upon me that afternoon one of those oppressions of the spirit that never weigh so heavily as when they visit you in the full tide of health, under the wide and kindly sky. How shall one account for the apprehensions that crowd upon you, and seem not to have their birth within? In what subtle way does the universe convey the knowledge that it has ceased to be friendly? Even in the full sunlight, the idea of spending a night there alone was unwelcome.

"Soon after arriving I had despatched my men to La Galette for supplies, as we did today, but the distance is shorter by the old

Chemin de Canot trail, and they should easily return before sunset. Although knowing this well, and that nothing but serious mischance would detain them, it was with a very definite sense of uneasiness that I watched the canoe cross the lake, saw them disembark, and in a few seconds disappear.

"The afternoon wore away in little occupations about the camp, and in fishing along the shore; later on I intended to scramble around the edge of the lake to the canoe, and try casting in the middle. Out there, quite beyond the reach of my flies, one tremendous rise showed that Duchêne's stories were not wholly fables, and when evening fell there might be a chance to prove them true. But this fortune was not for me; another must discover the secrets of that mysterious water.

"Already the barometer had shown that a swift change of weather was at hand; gradually, and scarcely perceptibly, the ever-thickening veil of cirrus mist dimmed the brightness of the sun, until, pale and lifeless, it disappeared in tumultuous clouds that rose to meet it. As the storm came rapidly on, it seemed to me, in the utter stillness, that I could hear the rush of the vapours writhing overhead. Then with a roar that fairly cowed the soul, the wind, leaping up the mountain side, fell upon the little habitation, and would have carried it away had my whole weight not been thrown against the tent pole. In the darkness that drew like a curtain across the sky I waited miserably, dreading I knew not what, beyond the gale and the javelins of the lightning.

"Sitting with an arm around the pole I heard, through the wind and the rain, a cry. Even answering it, I doubted that it was human; when it came again I tried to think that some solitary loon was calling to his familiar spirits of the storm. Never have I passed such an hour under canvas. The wind had the note you hear in a gale of sea. Lightning showed the surface of the lake torn into spindrift that was swept across it like rank on rank of sheeted ghosts. The thunder seemed to have its dwelling-place in both earth and sky.

"In a lull to gather force for a fresh assault, the cry again: again, and nearer, when the wind burst upon the mountaintop, as though released from some mighty dam in the heavens. This was not voice of beast or bird, and courage fell from me like a garment. The numbness of terror possessed me; I sat with nails digging into the wood, saying over and over some silly rhyme. Close at hand the cry — heart-breaking, dreadful, unbearable ...

"Wrenching myself free, as from the grip of a nightmare, I leaped to the door of the tent; five paces away in the howling blackness stood something in the form of a man, and in one stricken moment the lightning revealed what I would give much that is dear to blot from memory. As the creature sprang, with its hellish voice filling my ears, I flung into the water, diving far and deep. Swimming with frantic strokes for the farther shore, I did not, in the greater fear, bethink me that this indeed was the Lake of Hell. The pursuing cry, rising ever and anon above all other sounds, kept nerve and muscle strung in the agony of the desire to escape. Crawling out exhausted and breathless, but stopping no instant, I plunged down the mountain-side — staggering, falling, clutching, somehow I reached the bottom, and pitched into a bed of moss, like an animal shot through the neck.

"When I could breathe and feel and hear again, my ears caught only the sounds of the retreating storm and of a rapid on the river. Stumbling painfully towards it, I saw with inexpressible joy the light of a fire, where my men had camped when overtaken by darkness and the tempest.

"The next day I went out of the woods, the men returning to bring in tent and canoe. They met with nothing, but I don't believe that their heart was in the search."

"And what in God's name was it?"

"Pray Him it was not poor Duchêne in the flesh."

This page intentionally left blank

T H E   W I N D I G O

by
W.H. Drummond
from *Dr. W.H. Drummond's Complete Poems*. Toronto: McClelland
& Stewart, 1926.

The Wendigo is an ominous presence in the forests of Canada's North and one cannot be too careful when the spirits crawl and roam during the Hour of the Wolf.

This page intentionally left blank

Go easy wit' de paddle, an' steady wit' de
oar
Geev rudder to de bes' man you got among de
crew,
Let ev'ry wan be quiet, don't let dem sing no
more
W'en you see de islan' risin' out of Grande
Lac Manitou.

Above us on de sky dere, de summer cloud may
Float
Aroun' us on de water de ripple never show,
But somet'ing down below us can rock de
stronges' boat,
W'en we're comin' near de islan' of de spirit
Windigo!

De carcajou may breed dere, an' otter sweem de
pool
De moosh-rat mak' de mud house, an' beaver
buil' hees dam
An' beeges' Injun hunter on all de Tête de Boule
Will never set hees trap dere from spring to
summer tam.

But he'll bring de fines' presen' from upper St.
Maurice
De loup marin an' black-fox from off de Hod-
son Bay
An' hide dem on de islan' an' smoke de pipe of
peace.
So Windigo will help heem w'en he travel far
away.
We shaintee on dat islan' on de winter seexty-
nine
If you look you see de clearin' aroun' de Coo
Coo Cache,
An' pleasan' place enough too among de spruce
an' pine
If foreman on de shaintee is n't Cyprien
Palache.

Beeg feller, always wat chin' on hees leetle weasel
Eye,
De gang dey can't do not'ing but he see dem
purty quick
Wit' hees "Hi dere, w'at you doin'?" ev'ry tam
he's passin' by
An' de bad word he was usin', wall! it offen
mak' me sick.

An' he carry silver w'issle wit' de chain aroun'
hees neck
For fear he mebbe los' it, an' ev'rybody
say
He mus' buy it from de devil w'en he's passin'
on Kebeck

But if it's true dat story, I dunno how moche
        he pay.

Dere's plaintee on de shaintee can sing lak ros-
        signol
Pat Clancy play de fiddle, an' Jimmie Char-
        bonneau
Was bring hees concertina from below St.
        Fereol
So we get some leetle pleasure till de long,
        long winter go.

But if we start up singin' affer supper on de
        camp.
"Par derriere chez ma tante," or "Mattawa
        wishtay,"
De boss he'll come along den, an' put heem out
        de lamp,
An' only stop hees swearin' w'en we all go
        marche coucher.

We've leetle boy dat winter from Po-po-lo-be-
        lang
Hees fader an' hees moder dey're bote
        A-ben-a-kee
An' he's comin', Injun Johnnie, wit' some man
        de lumber gang
Was fin' heem nearly starvin' above on Lac
        Souris.

De ole man an' de woman is tryin' pass de Soo
W'en water's high on spring tam, an' of course
        dey're getting' drown',
For even smartes' Injun should n't fool wit'
        birch canoe,
W'ere de reever lak toboggan on de hill is
        runnin' down.

So dey lef' de leetle feller all alone away up
        dere

Till lumber gang is ketchin' him an' bring him
          on de Cache,
But better if he's stayin' wit' de wolf an' wit'
          de bear
Dan come an' tak' hees chances wit' Cyprien
          Palache.

I wonder how he stan' it, w'y he never run
          away
For Cyprien lak neeger he is treat heem all
          de sam'
An' if he's wantin' Johnnie on de night or on de
          day
God help heem if dat w'issle she was below de
          secon' tam!

De boy he don't say not'ing, no wan never see
          heem cry
He's got de Injun in heem, you can see it on
          de face,
An' only for us feller an' de cook, he'll surely
          die
Long before de winter's over, long before we
          lef' de place,
But I see heem hidin' somet'ing wan morning
          by de shore
So firse tam I was passin' I scrape away de
          snow
An' it's rabbit skin he's ketchin' on de swamp
          de day before,
Leetle Injun Johnnie's workin' on de spirit
          Windigo.

December's come in stormy, an' de snow-dreef
          fill de road
Can only see de chimley an' roof of our cabane,
An' stronges' team in stable fin' it plaintee
          heavy load
Haulin' sleigh an' two t'ree pine log t'roo de
          wood an' beeg savane.

An' I travel off wan day me, wit' Cyprien
Palache,
Explorin' for new timber, w'en de win' begin
to blow,
So we hurry on de snow-shoe for de camp on Coo
Coo Cache
If de nor' eas' storm is comin', was de bes'
place we dunno —

An' we're getting' safe enough dere wit' de storm
close on our heel,
But w'en our belt we loosen for takin' off de
coat
De foreman commence screamin' an' mon Dieu
it mak' us feel
Lak he got t'ree t'ousan' devil all fightin' on
hees t'roat.

Cyprien is los' hees w'issle, Cyprien is los' hees
chain
Injun Johnnie he mus' fin' it, even if de win'
is high
He can never show hese'f on de Coo Coo Cache
again
Till he bring dat silver w'issle an' de chain it's
hangin' by.

So he sen' heem on hees journey never knowin'
he come back
T'roo de rough an' stormy wedder, t'roo de
pile of dreefin' snow
"Wat's de use of bein' Injun if you can't smell
out de track?"
Dat's de way de boss is talkin', an' poor
Johnnie have to go.

If you want to hear de musique of de nort' win'
as it blow
An' lissen to de hurricane an' learn de way it
sing

An' feel how small de man is w'en he's leevin'
here below,
You should try it on de shaintee w'en she's
doin' all dem t'ing!

W'at's dat soun' lak somet'ing cryin' all aroun'
us ev'ryw'ere?
We never hear no toner upon de winter
storm!
Dey're shoutin' to each oder dem voices on de
air,
An' it's red hot too de stove pipe, but no
wan's feelin' warm!

"Get out an' go de woodpile before I freeze to
deat"
Cyprien de boss is yellin' an' he's lookin' cole
an' w'ite
Lak dead man on de coffin, but no wan go, you
bet,
For if it's near de woodpile, 't is n't close
enough to-night!

Non! we ain't afraid of not'ing, but we don't
lak takin' chance,
An' w'en we hear de spirit of de wil' A-ben-a-
kee
Singin' war song on de chimley, makin' all dem
Injun dance
Raisin' row dere, you don't ketch us on no
woodpile — no siree!

O! de lonesome night we're passin' w'ile we're
stayin' on dat place!
An' ev'rybody sheever w'en Jimmie Char-
bonneau
Say he's watchin' on de winder an' he see de
Injun face
An' it's lookin' so he tole us, jus' de sam' as
Windigo.

Den again mese'f I'm hearin' somet'ing callin',
an' it soun'
Lak de voice of leetle Johnnie so I'm passin'
on de door
But de pine stump on de clearin' wit' de w'ite
sheet all aroun'
Mak' me t'ink of churchyar' tombstone, an'
I can't go dere no more.

Wat's de reason we're so quiet w'ile out heart
she's goin' fas'
W'y is no wan ax de question? dat we're all
afraid to spik?
Was it wing of flyin' wil' bird strek de winder as
it pass,
Or de sweesh of leetle snow-ball w'en de win'
is playing' trick?

W'en we buil' de Coo Coo shaintee, she's as
steady as a rock,
Did you feel de shaintee shakin' de sam, she's
goin' to fall?
Dere's somet'ing on de doorway! an' now we
hear de knock
An' up above de hurricane we hear de w'issle
call.
Callin', callin' lak a bugle, an' he's jompin' up
de boss
From hees warm bed on de corner an' open
wide de door —
Dere's no use foller affer for Cyprien is los'
An' de Coo Coo Cache an' shaintee he'll
never see no more.

At las' de morning's comin', an' storm is blow
away
An' outside on de shaintee young Jimmie
Charbonneau
He's seein' track of snowshoe, 'bout de size of
double sleigh

Dere's no mistak' it's makin' by de spirit
Windigo.

An' de leetle Injun Johnnie, he's all right I
onderstan'
For you'll fin' heem up de reever above de
Coo Coo Cache
Ketchin' mink and ketchin' beaver, an' he's
growin' great beeg man
But dat's de las' we're hearin' of Cyprien
Palache.

WHEN WIRES ARE DOWN

by
Lillian Benyon Thomas
from *The Thrill Book*, September 1, 1919.

This would have been a story to read in the club car of the westbound CPR Transcontinental as it pulled out of Winnipeg and into the night toward the Prairies.

This page intentionally left blank

"Speakin' of spirits and the angels at Mons, and all them kind of things, I don't believe in none of it," the mail carrier said.

No one had mentioned spirits or the angels at Mons, and I sat up suddenly, for I was at that minute trying to read by the flickering lamp of the one lamp in the station waiting room, an article on the great revival of interest in spiritualism that the war had occasioned.

"Strange that you mentioned that now," the agent said in a husky, disgruntled voice, for he was suffering from the flu, which had settled in his throat and his mental outlook on life.

He was half lying on his desk in the inner office, and without raising his head from his arms, he mumbled: "One of the fellows was telling me today that Simpson left because this station is haunted."

"I've heard that yarn," the mail carrier replied with evident disgust, and he projected a great wad of tobacco toward a cuspidor that stood to the right of the stove, surrounded by the well-intentioned, but overreaching or too weak efforts of a careless public; "but if it had been haunted I'd have seen something of it, for I've been here every night for five years. There may be spirits in the world, I don't say there ain't; but when a fellow begins to tell me he has been seein' signs, and gettin' messages, I asks him what he's been eatin' and drinkin'. It's what's inside, I says, not outside that is makin' the trouble."

"Simpson didn't drink too much," the agent mumbled.

"Naw!" the mail carrier agreed as he pushed mail bags out of his way with the toe of his boot and tilted his chair back until he could raise his feet to the ledge around the centre of the stove. "Simpson was city bred, that was what was the matter with him; he got lonesome. He imagined the wind in the telegraph wires was voices, and just ordinary silence was to him a terrible hush. When there was a blizzard ragin' on the prairie the way there is tonight, and the wires got down both goin' and comin', he began to think how far he was from home and friends and got panicky; and when you get that way, you see can see and hear things as never was."

The agent shoved back his chair, and it made a screeching sound on the floor of the inner office. He buttoned his grey sweater around him, put on his coat and fastened it up close to his throat, put on his cap and pulled it down over his ears, and came out into the general waiting room.

He stopped a minute at the stove, which looked like a tippler who is so far gone he does not care for his personal appearance. It was dribbled with ashes all the way down its neglected front; its top and bottom showed some signs of having once been black, but its belly was a faded grey, with a faint reddish glow in one spot in the back that showed there was some life within.

The agent extended his hands over the stove and shivered slightly as those do affected with the flu. Then he reached for the coal scuttle that was half full of coal. It had a small shovel in it, and with the shovel he opened the stove door, then stooped down to the scuttle and made a great rattling among the coal, trying to fill the shovel and carry it full to the stove; but much of it fell back, and much dribbled on to the floor, and scattered in all directions. I noticed two pieces that rolled until they hit a door back of the stove, a door that gave back a hollow sound.

The agent was too ill to gather them up. He slammed the stove door shut with the shovel and when it did not catch, being clogged with ashes, he kicked it with the sole of his boot until it did. Then he went to the door leading to the platform and opened it carefully, but the storm that was raging outside came through with such force that it knocked him back and took away his breath.

He tugged at the door to get it closed after him, but it was not until the mail carrier got up and put his shoulder to it that the catch finally caught and stayed.

I was sitting on a bench beside the wall on the same side as the station platform door and I noticed how the tables and calendars and exhibition announcements on the walls rattled and swung backward and forward.

A big Massey-Harris calendar featuring a harvesting combine on the back of the door on the opposite side of the room from me blew down and I got up and picked it up and hung it back on the door.

I noticed as I did so that stripping had at some time been nailed around the door to keep out the wind, but it looked dusty and settled, like a door that is not used.

After hanging the harvester company calendar back on its nail, I returned to my seat; the agent came in and, after another fight with the wind, succeeded in shutting the door with a bang that sent such a gust of air through the room that again the calendars and time-tables rattled, and the light in the one lamp that was in a bracket near the ticket wicket, bounded out of the top of the chimney and went out in a burst of smoke.

We were not in complete darkness, for there was a slight glow from the stove; and the ticket wicket and the door into the inner office were both open, and the light in there, while it danced and flickered, did not go out.

The mail carrier got up and reached for the lamp in the bracket, while with his other hand he struck a match on the seat of his trousers. The agent went on into the inner office.

"Any sign of her?" I asked him.

The train was already three hours late and it was almost midnight.

"Not a sign," he said, "and it's a terrible night — like Hell let loose — I pity any one who is out tonight."

"It was just such a night as this that a woman out in the country was frozen to death," the mail carrier said.

Not desiring to hear any tales of horror, such as are popular amongst the people who do the waiting work of the world, I got up and went to the wicket and asked: "Can you find out where she is? Has she left Brandon yet?"

"Can't tell you a thing about her," he said. "The wires are down. She may be cancelled."

"It's a bad time of year to be travelling," the mail carrier continued. "Last week Simpson and a traveller like yourself, sir, and I waited here until four o'clock in the morning, and then the traveller gave up and went back to the hotel, and didn't she come through at four-thirty, and it was important for him to get to Winnipeg that night, too."

He waited for me to ask a question, but when I didn't, he continued: "He was a detective, working on the Morrison case — that was the one I mentioned — it was Mrs. Morrison who was frozen to death."

"Oh," I said. "How was that?" I found myself sitting up rather straight.

"I guess you saw it in the papers — you did if you belong in these parts." He waited for me to enlighten him, but when I didn't he asked: "You don't belong here do you?"

"No!" I answered.

"Just came in at noon, didn't you?" he continued with the curiosity of one whose chief interest in life is the casual traveller, who is rather rare at such little stations as Oakhom, in the middle of a Manitoba winter.

"Yes," I said.

"Ever been here before?" he asked with frank curiosity.

"No," I said. "Never before."

"Morrison was a farmer," he continued, returning to his story. "I lived on his homestead about ten miles from here. I didn't know him — nobody knew much about him — he lived pretty much to himself. Some people said Morrison wasn't his name, he was hidin', I don't know. But he disappeared three weeks ago and nothin' has been seen or heard of him since."

"He has likely gone to visit friends or to see the world," I said. "No doubt he'll turn up before Spring."

"I'd say that too, if there hadn't been somethin' mysterious about his disappearance," he explained.

He was still holding the lamp in his hand, but he turned to put it up in the bracket, and as I watched him, I was conscious of something moving behind him.

I peered into the shadows with some surprise, for I thought there were only the three of us in the station waiting room; and I had not seen a cat or dog or anything else alive, and no one could come in from outside without an accompaniment of wind and snow.

The mail carrier returned to his seat, and I saw that it was the calendar I had hung on the door opposite that I had seen moving. It was swaying forward as if impelled by a gentle, but constant wind.

I recalled that as I had felt up and down the door to find the nail on which to hang the calendar I had thought it seemed more solid than the usual softwood doors in such places.

"What is there mysterious about a man going away for a few weeks in the middle of winter?" I asked absently, my eyes still on the calendar.

"Morrison did his business and got his mail at a small town on the CN line," the mail carrier continued, "but six weeks ago he came over here and left a sealed envelope with the lawyer. He would not explain anything, but he told the lawyer that he would report to him every Monday, and if he missed a Monday the lawyer was to open the envelope and follow the instructions given inside. The lawyer thought him a bit queer, but promised to do as he wished."

"Sounds mysterious!" I said when he paused for effect.

He paused so long that I noticed how the elements were tearing at the little station house. It was like some wild beast worrying it until it creaked and groaned in protest — and all the while the wind was playing some wild dirge on the frosty wires — something that did not seem of earth or things human.

"A bad night," the mail carrier said, as the wind beat against the window. "But that night was worse, the night she was frozen to death. But I was speaking about Morrison. He called to see the lawyer for three Mondays, then he missed. The lawyer opened the envelope."

The agent got up and came into the general waiting room and stood beside the stove. He was a newcomer and he had evidently not heard the story.

"Morrison stated that his life was in danger, and that a search was to be started for him at once. He said they were to look for him and a man who wore a gold ring with a peculiar crest on it. He gave a rough sketch of the crest. It was heart-shaped, with two crossed keys in the centre."

"Was there no clue to his disappearance?"

"No and yes," the mail carrier answered ponderously. "When Morrison came to his farm his wife was with him — a young bit of a girl who didn't know any more about a farm than I do about a machine gun, and not as much I guess. The neighbours said she was much above him — educated and accomplished and all that — and he was ignorant and coarse. I don't know why, no one does, but he and his wife did not seem to get along from the first, and it was on a night like this that she started for a neighbour's in her night clothes. She was frozen to death of course. He said she walked in her sleep — no one will ever know."

I felt my hands twitching — closing and unclosing spasmodically — it was such a terrible night for a young bit of a girl, all alone on the prairie.

"A strange story!" I said.

"Yes," he agreed, and paused again like one who has yet more startling things to tell.

"Yes, and the neighbours say his wife had a gold ring with a heart-shaped crest, with two crossed keys in the centre."

"What is their explanation?"

"Some say they belonged to a secret society, maybe spies hidin'; some say she belonged to a titled family and ran away with him; and some say she wasn't his wife, that she was married to another man, but," — he paused — "it's all gossip; nobody knows."

I pulled my cap down over my eyes and picked up my gloves that were on the seat beside me and put the one on my left hand — then I glanced around in a casual way to see if others were watching me.

I suddenly sat bolt upright, my eyes almost popping out of my head, for on the bench, on the opposite side of the room, a man, evidently a farmer, sat huddled up, his legs drawn in under the seat, his arms hanging stiffly down at his side, his whole appearance that of a man too ill to care for anything.

He wore a sheepskin coat, a nondescript cap of some kind, and a muffler around the upturned collar of his coat. His cap was drawn down over his ears and forehead until only his eyes were visible — and there was something grotesque in his appearance — caused I decided by a projecting end of his muffler that stuck up back of his head like a cord to hang a picture or a statue.

The mail carrier was still talking to me and when I did not

answer, he looked at me, and then his eyes followed the direction of mine. His feet and his chair came to the floor suddenly with a bang.

"By gosh! how did you get in? I didn't hear you."

The stranger did not answer, but seemed to sag down like one too utterly weary to bother.

"The flu?" the mail carrier asked sympathetically, after a pause, when the stranger did not move or speak.

The agent beckoned me to go into the inner office.

"When did he come in?" he asked in a low voice when we were beside his desk.

"I don't know," I said. "I had no idea any one had come in until I saw him sitting there."

"He didn't come through that door," he said, and nodded toward the door leading to the station platform. "No one can come in that way tonight without creating a commotion."

"He must have come through that door," I said, and nodded toward a door in the inner office.

"No he didn't," the agent said decidedly. "I locked that door when I brought in the coal. Tramps might get in and set fire to the place."

He evidently wanted me to believe that it was not fear that made him lock the door.

"There is another door into the waiting room," I said, and looked toward the door on which I had hung the calendar.

"He must have come in that way," the agent agreed. "I'll see that it is locked. No one else will come through there while I'm here!"

He went out and tried the door.

It resisted.

There was a key in the lock and he tried to turn it. He looked over at me and said, "It is locked."

He came back into the inner office. "He must have locked it when he came in, but he'll get out before I leave tonight. This is not going to be a hotel for tramps."

I could see that the stranger was getting on his nerves, for no one would turn a man out on such a night.

The mail carrier had been watching us, but when I returned to my seat in the outer office, he turned to the stranger again and said, "The flu?"

The man appeared to nod in affirmation, but the mail carrier had not fitted the lamp properly into the bracket, and the flame was turned against the side of the chimney, which was already black and smoked, and I could not be sure that the stranger had moved.

"I know what the flu is," the mail carrier continued, and then paused.

Everything was suddenly as still as on the calmest summer day. Prairie dwellers all know those pauses that come in even the worst storms, when the elements seem to take a second or two to get their breath, only to come back in renewed fury.

We waited to hear again the whistle and scream of the wind, but instead we heard the soft distant tones of a pipe organ. It was on the other side of the door opposite me — the door on which I had hung the calendar — at first low, then gaining in power and volume as it seemed to approach, until it seemed that we were beside it; and we recognized the grand but solemn music of the dead march.

The agent, who was still in the inner office, came to the wicket and looked out at us; the mail carrier sat up very straight, with a plug of black tobacco from which he had been taking chews all night halfway to his mouth; and I rose to my feet, but the man in the corner did not move. I looked to see if he had noticed it, and I felt suddenly that there was something familiar about him.

"By gosh, it sounded like an organ!" the mail carrier said, when the wind came again in a rush and tore at the building, snarling as a dog snarls when it shakes a rat.

"It sounded like the dead march to me," the agent said, and returned to his chair.

"There isn't a pipe organ within two hundred miles, and not an organ of any kind nearer than the village, and that's half a mile away, and you couldn't hear it fifty yards," the mail carrier declared.

Something made me look again toward the calendar I had hung on the door opposite. It was doubtless the fact that it was still blowing forward.

"What is on the other side of that door?" I asked the mail carrier.

"That is a freight shed, but it has never been used. It has never been needed, so it was nailed up."

"It must be a drafty place," I said. "Look at the way that calendar is blowing."

He looked at it for a few seconds steadily — then looked away — like one who distrusts his eyes, then back again.

I noticed that the calendar made a still greater angle with the door.

The mail carrier got up deliberately and went to the door opposite and felt under and around the calendar. He felt up and down the cracks where the stripping had been nailed and then he shook his head.

He pushed the calendar back against the door with his hand, but when he released it, it returned to its former position.

"By gosh!" he said, and he stood back and looked at it.

Something in his tone brought the agent to his feet. He came to the door of his office, which was quite near the door on which the calendar hung.

"What is it?" he asked.

"Look at that calendar."

"There must be a terrific wind through that place," the agent said, after looking at it.

"Come and feel!" the mail carrier suggested.

The agent reached out and felt under the calendar and up and down and around it — then he looked at the mail carrier — and then they both turned and looked at me.

I went over and felt around the door as they had done, but, as I expected, I could not feel the slightest draft; the door seemed singularly solid.

"I swan!" the agent ejaculated.

"By gosh!" the mail carrier said again.

I did not say anything, but nodded toward the calendar, that had again defied all laws of gravity — and was hanging in a horizontal position, making two right angles with the door.

I went to it, put my two hands on it, and pushed it down.

It yielded as a feather bed yields, but returned to a horizontal position when I removed my hands.

"The place is haunted!" the agent said, and glanced toward the huddled figure in the corner, but the man appeared to be too ill to care even for ghosts.

I could see his eyes and they were fixed and starey, like the eyes of one who is very ill or asleep with but half-shut eyes. I wondered what it was about him that made him seem vaguely familiar.

"I've been here every night for five years," the mail carrier said skeptically, "and if this place is haunted I'd know something about it."

He went to the door, took the calendar from the nail and put it on the floor. It lay where it was put like an ordinary calendar.

The agent took a calendar from the door leading into his office and hung it on the door of the freight shed. It remained still a second, then began to rise.

"It's electricity," the mail carrier said. "It's electricity and there is —"

He stopped suddenly for again there was the peculiar hush that had preceded the organ music. It may have been that our nerves were unstrung, but it seemed to me to be a more intense hush than the usual lull in a storm and also that there was something expectant and ominous about it.

Instinctively I stepped forward and stood between the agent and the mail carrier and closer to them.

We stood facing the door leading into the freight shed, and I shivered when I saw the calendar sink slowly back into a normal position; and icy fingers seemed to play up and down my spine.

Again it began at a distance, on the other side of the door, on the far side of the unused freight shed.

It sounded at first like some one shovelling coal, but the coal scuttle was still beside the stove with the shovel in it.

Soon it seemed that some one was dumping a whole load of coal on the other side of the door — and we could hear the odd pieces rolling quite up to the other side of the door, until it seemed the ones the agent had dropped on our side had just come through.

Then there was a great crash, as if a whole carload of coal had suddenly been backed up against the shed and was all being dumped at once on the other side of the door.

We shrank back at the onrush of the great mass that we knew the door could not withstand. On it came like thunder and hurled itself against the freight-shed door.

The door did not yield — the calendar did not even tremble — we felt no physical shock from the impact; and the wind was again whistling and sighing at the desolate little station house.

"My God, what is it?" I asked. I am not a coward, but it was getting on my nerves. I could see that the other two men were also badly shaken up.

The huddled figure in the corner had not moved, but instead of being a comfort to us, for there is always comfort in numbers at such a time, the man with the grotesque handle at the back of his neck, his queer starey eyes, and general air of illness and remoteness, added to our discomfort.

"They say these things go in threes," the agent said, and I could see even in the wavering light that he was very pale.

"I don't believe it," the mail carrier said, but his tone did not carry conviction.

"It is the third day, of the third month, of the third year of the war," I said, thinking out all the threes I could as I went along.

"It is the third day of this storm; the third train that has been so late; and the third time three of us have waited here nearly all night," the mail carrier said, then added with a zest for the gruesome, "the third month since Morrison's wife was frozen to death, and the third week since he disappeared."

I glanced toward the huddled figure in the corner, when he spoke of three of us waiting for the train.

"He might as well not be there for all the good he is," he said in an undertone. "He seems half asleep all the time."

We stood around the stove a few minutes in silence. It was the mail carrier who spoke.

"I am going to open that door," he said. Some one has been dumping a carload of coal."

"But there is no coal here," the agent said. "I would know if there was any coal at this station."

"It must have been here before you came, or just came in to-night, or something," the mail carrier insisted, and went toward the door.

I instinctively put out my hand to stop him, and I saw the agent do the same; but we did not care to be thought cowards, so we said nothing.

He went to the door.

It seemed to me that he stepped more firmly and heavily than necessary.

He did not hesitate, but turned the knob, and pulled.

I confess that every separate hair on my head and body seemed to have come to life, and was standing at attention; and I was not sorry when the door resisted.

The key was in the lock and the mail carrier turned it. The lock went back with a dull thud. I shivered and I noticed that the agent was standing very tense.

The mail carrier pulled on the door again — he jerked it — but still it resisted.

"It is nailed up on the other side," he said, and looked back over his shoulder at us.

There was a queer hollow chuckle — not human — not like anything we had ever heard — we all looked toward the man in the corner, but he had not moved. Again I felt the irritation of something familiar about him that I could not account for.

"What are you chuckling about?" the mail carrier demanded, and advanced toward him. "Why don't you get up and help find out what is making the trouble if you know so much about it?"

The mail carrier's nerves were beginning to feel the strain.

I do not know what he would have done to the huddled figure in the corner, if at that second the terrible hush had not come upon us a third time.

If you have ever waited at a death-bed in the stillness of the night — alone with the soul that is getting ready for flight — you know something of how we felt. Our bodies were tense, our faces white and strained, and I recalled afterward how the eyes of the mail carrier and the agent stood almost out of their sockets.

The silence lasted so long that I thought I would scream — that I must do something to break the spell — when on the far side of the shed, on the other side of the door, we heard footsteps.

There could be no doubt about it — they were stealthy, stealing, menacing steps, and they were coming toward the door behind which we stood.

We were held like people in a nightmare, who feel the approach of something more than human intelligence can bear.

The steps stopped — we listened — they came stealing on again, nearer and nearer.

Across the big freight shed we heard them approaching closer and closer, until they were just on the other side of the door — and then they stopped.

The hush continued; and then I saw the knob of the door turn. I made a queer sound in my throat.

The door began to open as stealthily as the knob had been turned — slowly and silently.

I sprang toward it.

"Hold it! Hold it!" I screamed, or I think I screamed. The others said I made no sound, but they sprang with me.

We put all our strength against it. We pushed and strained.

It opened as resistlessly as the raging storm outside; we were shoved back slowly, steadily, silently.

Inch by inch the door opened, and inch by inch we yielded.

At last it was open, and we saw thick dust undisturbed on the floor — cobwebs hanging from rafters and walls; nothing human had crossed the threshold of that door for months, possibly years.

It was the mail carrier who went into the inner office and brought out a trainman's lantern, one with a strong reflector that threw a clear light ahead.

I stood at his right, the agent at his left, as he turned the light of the lantern into the freight shed.

I do not know who made a queer gurgling sound, or groaned, or gasped; but all those sounds were made, as the light of the lantern fell on a queer, huddled-up figure in a sheepskin coat, with its legs bent under it; its arms hanging down stiffly at its sides; its cap drawn down over its ears and forehead until only its eyes, starey and fixed, were visible; and the projecting end of something stuck up back of its head, like a cord to hang a picture or statue.

My eyes followed the projecting end of the cord up and up, and from the low rafter above there dangled the other end of a cord.

As one man we turned and looked into the corner where the stranger was sitting.

He was not there.

We looked around the room. There was no one in the waiting room, but the mail carrier, the station agent, and myself.

It was the agent who, with a panting sound, caught the door and slammed it shut.

It was the mail carrier who fumbled at the key until he turned it, and the lock went back into place with a dull thud.

I saw that their faces looked like the faces of men who have seen things for which men have no words.

I do not know how long we stood there, the wind tearing at the building, the snow beating against the windows, the telegraph wires shrieking and moaning and groaning in protest against something they did not understand — it seemed an eternity; but it was not yet one o'clock when there was a shuffling sound on the station platform, the door was opened, and a man in a long coonskin coat entered.

He struggled with the door and finally succeeded in getting it shut; then he looked at us.

"Why, what's the matter? Has anything happened?" he asked.

No one answered him.

"You all look as if you had seen a ghost," he said.

"We have. We've been spending the night with one," the mail carrier said.

"You talking about ghosts," the man laughed. "We'll begin to think the place is haunted if you talk like that."

"Don't laugh, doctor," the mail carrier said solemnly, "it's in there." He nodded toward the shed. "But it spent the night on that bench," and he pointed to the corner where it had been.

"What are you talking about?" the man called the doctor asked.

"Look in there and see," the mail carrier answered, and handed him the lantern.

We all stood back of him — we did not wish to look in again — but we knew we would.

The doctor took the lantern and opened the door that yielded readily to him, and looked into the freight shed.

"My God!" he gasped when his eyes fell on the thing. "It's a man!"

He looked intently at it without stepping over the threshold of the door, for a long time, then he turned toward us and said: "It's Morrison! That's who it is! It's Morrison!"

He looked again, still without stepping over the threshold of the door, and twisted the lantern to get different views. He turned toward us again.

"Yes, it's Morrison! Looks like a case of suicide! I guess the poor devil was a bit off his balance; the loss of his wife and all that. That letter about being threatened by a person with a peculiar ring sounded queer. No one with a crest has been in these parts."

He closed the door carefully, locked it, and put the key in his pocket. "I'll get the coroner in the morning."

"That doesn't explain how he came to be sitting in that corner all night," the mail carrier said, and pointed toward the corner.

"You've ben eating something that disagreed with you," the doctor answered good-naturedly.

"We haven't all been eatin' somethin' that disagreed with us," the mail carrier insisted, "and we all saw it, didn't we?"

We corroborated his statement; but the agent was new to the place, and I was a stranger, just there for the day.

"Then I guess you've all been drinking the same thing," the doctor said skeptically. He looked at me sharply and asked: "You were asking for Morrison today?"

"Yes, I came out to see him on business," I replied.

"Didn't you recognize him tonight?" he asked.

"No, it is some years since I saw him, and he had changed."

"Yes, he had," the doctor said reminiscently. "I remember him when he came. He looked a lot younger. Did he owe you anything?"

"No, I owed him something, but I find he has cancelled the debt."

At that moment we heard the long-delayed train.

I took my grips and got on board.

Fortunately, I had reserved a berth in the Pullman — but I got on the day coach, and sat there until the train started.

Then I took my grips and started back though the train; but when I reached the platform of the day coach, I put down my grips and removed my gloves.

From the little finger of my left hand I drew a ring, which I took between the finger and thumb of my right hand, and threw as far as I could out into the ice and snow — somewhere between Oakhom and Winnipeg.

It was a gold ring, with a heart-shaped crest, and crossed keys in the centre.

I went into the Pullman and put my grips in my berth, but I did not feel like sleep, so went into the smoking room; to my surprise I found it occupied by a soldier.

He told me he had been at the front for two years.

"What do you think of that story about the angels at Mons?" I asked.

"I can't exactly say," he replied with a tightening up of reserve, "although I was in that battle."

"Were there angels there?"

"I didn't see any."

"I am particularly interested," I explained, "because I had a peculiar experience today. I went out to Oakhom to find a man who did me a great injury. When I got there I heard he had disappeared in a mysterious way. I did not pay any attention to the mysterious part of it, for I thought he had heard I was on the way, and knew it was safer for him to get out. I felt certain that he would not return until I was at a safe distance, so after making arrangements with the lawyer to let me know if they heard anything about him, I went to the station to wait for the train."

I paused, and the soldier said, "Well!"

I told him what had happened. He listened without comment.

When I had finished, we sat in silence for a while. The train had stopped, the light flickered in the one lamp in the smoking room, and we could hear the storm beating and tearing at the train.

"I have lived on these prairies twenty years," he said, "and things I couldn't explain have happened, "but I don't think there is any mystery about what happened to you tonight."

"How would you explain it?" I asked.

"Farmers all look pretty much alike when wearing those sheepskin coats with their caps pulled down over their eyes. There is an epidemic of flu in the district, and I think that was a farmer who was too sick to be bothered talking."

"How did he get in?"

"He could have come in during a pause in the storm — you know it is perfectly calm at such times — and your attention was concentrated on the mail carrier's story; and doubtless he went out in disgust while you were watching that door."

"But the music, the coal, and the stealthy steps?"

"Listen!" he said.

I listened.

It seemed that I could hear queer sounds, almost like human moans around the train.

"A fellow imagines a lot," the soldier said.

"Yes," I agreed, "perhaps you are right."

"What is your explanation?" he asked.

"I haven't any," I said.

www.ingramcontent.com/pod-product-compliance
Lightning Source LLC
Chambersburg PA
CBHW030332020726
47493CB00004B/1250